When one night of passion leads to so much more...

How could she know that picking up a sexy stranger would turn her life upside down?

DANGEROUS
PASSION

LISA B. KAMPS

Lisa B. Kamps

DANGEROUS PASSION

Lisa B. Kamps

DANGEROUS PASSION

DANGEROUS PASSION
Copyright © 2016 by Elizabeth Belbot Kamps

All rights reserved. Except for use in any review, the reproduction or utilization of this work in whole or in part in any form by any electronic, mechanical or other means, now known or hereafter invented, including xerography, photocopying and recording, or in any information storage or retrieval system, is forbidden without the express written permission of the author.

All characters in this book have no existence outside the imagination of the author and have no relation to anyone bearing the same name or names, living or dead. This book is a work of fiction and any resemblance to any individual, place, business, or event is purely coincidental.

Photographer: CJC Photography
http://www.cjc-photography.com

Cover Model: BT Urruela
http://www.bturruela.com
http://www.vetsports.org

Artwork and Cover Design by Jay Aheer
Simply Defined Art
http://www.jayscoversbydesign.com/

Lisa B. Kamps

All rights reserved.
ISBN: 1539569306
ISBN-13: 978-1539569305

DANGEROUS PASSION

DEDICATION

For Michelle Monkou—my bestest buddy and BFF ever, forever. Thanks for having my back (always) and for pulling my can out of the fire!

DANGEROUS PASSION

Contents

Title Page iii
Copyright v
Dedication.. ix
Other titles by this author xv

Chapter One 19
Chapter Two... 27
Chapter Three 37
Chapter Four 50
Chapter Five 55
Chapter Six 62
Chapter Seven 68
Chapter Eight 74
Chapter Nine 86
Chapter Ten.. 98
Chapter Eleven 106
Chapter Twelve 112
Chapter Thirteen.. 119
Chapter Fourteen... 133
Chapter Fifteen 141
Chapter Sixteen.. 146
Chapter Seventeen 157
Chapter Eighteen 170
Chapter Nineteen... 180
Chapter Twenty 188
Chapter Twenty-One 196

Chapter Twenty-Two 202
Chapter Twenty-Three 209
Chapter Twenty-Four 219

ABOUT THE AUTHOR 233
ONCE BURNED preview 235

DANGEROUS PASSION

Lisa B. Kamps

Other titles by this author

THE BALTIMORE BANNERS

Crossing The Line, Book 1
Game Over, Book 2
Blue Ribbon Summer, Book 3
Body Check, Book 4
Break Away, Book 5
Playmaker (A Baltimore Banners Intermission novella)
Delay of Game, Book 6
Shoot Out, Book 7
The Baltimore Banners 1st Period Trilogy (Books 1-3)
On Thin Ice, Book 8
Coach's Challenge (A Baltimore Banners Intermission novella)
One-Timer, Book 9

FIREHOUSE FOURTEEN

Once Burned, Book 1
Playing With Fire, Book 2
Breaking Protocol, Book 3
Into The Flames, Book 4
Second Alarm, Book 5

STAND-ALONE TITLES

Emeralds and Gold: A Treasury of Irish Short Stories (*anthology*)
Finding Dr. Right, Silhouette Special Edition
Time To Heal
Dangerous Passion

Lisa B. Kamps

DANGEROUS PASSION

Lisa B. Kamps

Chapter One

Shelby Martin tightened her fingers on the nearly empty wine glass, wishing for a fleeting moment that the fragile stem was her friend's neck.

"How can you even say that?"

"It's the truth, Shel. You just skirt around the edges of life but you never get involved." Chrissy tossed back a colorful shot of something fun then offered her a brittle smile and a shrug. "Unless, of course, it's with your dusty collections."

Shelby forced her fingers to relax, afraid she really might snap the fragile glass in two, then took a sip of the chilled white wine as her mind raced for a comeback. Their other friend, Amanda, saved her from saying anything.

"At least she's not caught up in empty melodrama like someone else I know." Amanda raised her beer bottle to her lips and took a long swallow, then leaned closer to Shelby. "Don't pay attention to her, Shel. She's drunk. Again."

"No, I am not. And who cares if I am? I thought

the whole point of girl's night out was to cut loose and have some fun. But Miss Frigid here has put up a wall around us that's scaring all the men away."

"Chrissy, stop it."

"It's okay, Amanda, don't worry about it." Shelby forced a smile to her face then took another sip of her wine, its sweetness suddenly bitter on her tongue. The lighthearted banter from earlier was gone. A heavy silence settled over the trio, setting their table apart from the rowdy Friday night crowd gathered in the trendy Canton nightspot. Shelby fought the urge to glance down at her watch, wondering if she should just make up an excuse to go home. Chrissy must have sensed her intentions because she reached out and wrapped one slender hand around her wrist, pinning her in place.

"Shelby, I'm sorry. I was being a bitch. It's just...you used to be so much fun until that dickhead David dumped you. I always thought you could do better than him, but instead you just...you let him suck the life out of you. And even now that's he not in the picture, all you do is hide in your dusty building in your dusty office and play with your dusty collections—"

"Okay, Chrissy, I got your point. You don't need to go on like that." Shelby eased her arm from Chrissy's grip and hunched her shoulders around her ears, holding the wine glass between both hands. She *did* get Chrissy's point—which bothered her almost as much as the point Chrissy was making. Shelby dove head-first into her work, using it as a distraction from the break-up to the point that she let everything else pass her by. Now the break-up was ancient history—but Shelby's immersion in her work was even more consuming than before.

"Don't you just want to do something wild and crazy? Just, I don't know, pretend you're someone else? Just once?"

Shelby looked up at Chrissy and winced at the gleam she saw in her eyes. Coupled with the several shots Chrissy had already slammed back, the look could only mean trouble. Trouble for *Shelby*. Amanda's low groan confirmed her instinct.

But trouble or not, Chrissy's words stirred something to life in Shelby, a flicker of want, a spark of yearning. She didn't *want* to be so consumed by her work that she let everything else—let life—pass her by. But she didn't know to fix that, didn't know how to claw her way out of the dusty, boring existence that had become her life during the past three years.

Three years? Had it really been that long? Shelby frowned, absently sipping at the wine. More than that, actually. Since before she had started dating David. Or maybe just after that. When had it changed? Why had it changed? She was afraid she knew the answer to that—knew it, and didn't like it all. Which only made Chrissy's words more potent. More appealing.

Pretending to be someone she wasn't...yes, the temptation was as appealing as a ripe strawberry dipped in dark chocolate.

"Maybe. I mean, it's tempting but...I couldn't do it."

"What?" Amanda's surprised shock was drowned out by Chrissy's sudden excitement as she leaned forward and grabbed Shelby's wrist again.

"Yes you could. Just pretend the last few years never happened. You can do it, I know you can."

Shelby laughed, and even she could tell it sounded forced. She took another sip of the wine then sat back, eyeing Chrissy and ignoring Amanda's muttered warnings. "Okay, I'll try. So what do you want me to do? Match you shot for shot? Go get crazy on the dance floor? Pretend the two of us are a couple so you can get the guys to hit on you?" Shelby was pretty sure she could do any of those things—all she had to do was pretend the last few years had never happened, pretend that she hadn't really changed. The three of them used to do crazy things like that all the time together. It wouldn't be too difficult. At least, she didn't think it would.

But Chrissy was shaking her head with enough energy that strands of her blonde hair flew around her face. She impatiently brushed them away and grabbed Shelby's hand again. "No. You need to do something you've never done before. You need to pick out a guy and go have wild sex with him. *Tonight*."

"What? No. That's crazy."

"That's what you get for encouraging her."

"Amanda, stop. This is exactly what Shelby needs. And yes, Shel, it's crazy. That's the whole point. Look around. There's tons of gorgeous guys here. Just pick one and go. See what happens."

Shelby glanced around the crowded room. Yes, there were tons of guys here tonight. But not a single one stood out. Not a single one remotely struck her with the urge to walk over and strike up a conversation, let alone have a one-night stand with him.

A one-night stand. Oh dear Lord, what was she even thinking? She must really be losing her mind if she was sitting here even thinking about contemplating Chrissy's crazy words. She shook her head and turned back to face her friend.

"I'm sorry Chrissy, but that's not going to happen.

I can't. I'm not like you, I can't just go up to some stranger and—"

"Oh my God. *Him*. You have got to go talk to him."

"Who?" Shelby glanced around, trying to see who had caused the look of feral hunger in Chrissy's eyes. Amanda drew her breath in with a sharp hiss, which made Shelby turn in her seat and look behind her.

And she realized why her two friends were suddenly on high alert. Her own pulse kicked up several notches and she swore her face was heating as well.

The newcomer had just walked through the door and his presence was already drawing appreciative glances from the female occupants of the room. At first glance, Shelby thought he was tall and broad, but she blinked and realized that had been an illusion. Yes, he was a bit bigger than average, but not like she had first thought. No, it was his presence that made him seem larger than life.

And presence the man possessed. Just over six-feet tall, with broad shoulders, narrow waist, trim hips, and muscular legs. All packed into black leather and faded denim that hugged him in just the right spots. Shelby wanted to run her hands over the denim, to see if the material was as soft as it looked. To feel if his thighs were as hard as they looked.

She blinked again and let her eyes wander back up, pausing for a long second at waist-level before raking higher, appreciating the snug fit of the black polo shirt stretched tight across his chest. She would have loved to see his arms, to see if his biceps were as toned and muscular as she thought they must be, but they were encased in black leather, hidden by the motorcycle jacket he wore.

And Shelby realized that must be why he stood out in the crowd. It wasn't just his presence, the aura of power and authority and strength surrounding him, it was his clothes as well. He was the only one wearing jeans and motorcycle leather in a singles crowd of young professionals outdoing one another in a hapless effort to impress everyone else.

This man looked like he didn't care if he impressed anyone, as if he didn't care if he fit in or not.

Shelby's eyes drifted higher, finally resting on his face, and her pulse quickened even more. The slightest hint of beard shadowed his strong, square jaw; his dark hair was swept back off his face and curled just above the collar of the leather jacket. Coupled with his high cheekbones, he had a classic, rugged face that advertised adventure and screamed danger all at once. But his eyes...from where she sat, they looked dark in color. And intense. He shifted slightly, coming further into the club and surveying everything around him in one long sweep of the room.

Including her.

Shelby's heart paused as their gazes met in the briefest touch. Heat instantly filled her. Heat—and awareness. She swallowed and shifted in her seat, turning away from the searing touch of that all-too-brief look.

"Wow." Amanda turned around and fanned herself, a small grin on her face.

"Oh, yes." Chrissy's murmur was sly, determined. Her eyes remained glued to the newcomer long enough that Shelby had time to finish her wine in several long gulps. Chrissy finally pulled her gaze away and fixed Shelby with a long look. "If you don't talk to him, *I* will.

And if I have my way, we won't be talking for long."

Shelby stared at her friend, at her thick blonde hair and toned, voluptuous build, at the confidence that she wore like a cape, and opened her mouth to wish her luck.

And just as quickly, she snapped her mouth closed.

Chrissy, who never hesitated at taking chances.

Chrissy, who saw what she wanted and went after it.

Chrissy, who always had fun.

And Shelby suddenly wished *she* was the one who wasn't afraid to take chances and always have fun.

Chrissy gave her a pointed look, then held her hand up between them, raising her index finger.

One...

Was Shelby willing to take a chance?

Two...

Was Shelby willing to go after something she wanted and have fun?

Three...

Chrissy lowered her hand and shifted, ready to stand up. And Shelby knew if she did, that would be it. Her chance would be over. Chrissy would walk over to Mr. Tall, Dark, and Dangerous then walk out the door with him moments later.

Shelby slid out of the chair and stood so fast that she had to grab the back of it to keep it steady. Amanda turned and looked up at her, her brows furrowed in a funny combination of concern and surprise.

"Shelby! What are you doing? Are you insane?"

Insane. Yes, quite possibly. But Chrissy's earlier words came back to her. She *was* just skirting the edges of life. Tonight, she wanted to live.

But she had no idea what to do. Her grip tightened on the seat back and she looked quickly at Chrissy, silently asking for advice.

"Just go over and offer to buy him a drink. Flirt a little. See what kind of vibe you get from him."

"Chrissy, don't tell her that! He could be dangerous. He *looks* dangerous!"

"So she can trust her instincts. It's just a drink, for crying out loud. She doesn't *have* to leave with him." She turned back to face Shelby, raising her glass in a mock toast. "Just talk to him, see what happens. Follow your gut and do what feels right."

Do what feels right. Shelby nodded. She could do that. She glanced down at the empty wine glass and suddenly wished it was full. But then she realized she could order another one.

At the bar.

When she offered to buy the stranger a drink.

Shelby nodded and straightened, then took a deep breath and turned away from her friends.

To walk head-first into the dangerous heat of the unknown.

Chapter Two

Josh Nichols nodded to the bartender and motioned for a draft. The guy eyed him warily, then went about pouring his drink. Josh didn't blame the guy for being wary, not when he damn well knew who he was and what he did. Dressed like he was, Josh figured the bartender probably suspected he was working an undercover sting.

But he wasn't. Not tonight. At least, not anymore. He was officially off-duty, and had been for over an hour. Which was about eight hours too late, in his opinion.

He had no idea why he stopped at this particular club. Maybe because it was close by. Maybe because he knew he wouldn't run into anybody he knew here. He wanted anonymity tonight, wanted to lose himself in a crowd of strangers.

And yeah, maybe the idea of picking up a nameless, no-strings-attached, one-night-only deal had crossed his mind. He had already spotted a possible candidate, a buxom blonde sitting at a table near the entrance who looked like she wasn't afraid to have a little fun.

Spotted, then promptly discarded. There was too much melodrama surrounding that one and he knew that everything would be about her—and only her. Josh had no problems with pleasing any partner, enjoyed taking them to new heights, but sex was a two-way street in his opinion. He enjoyed giving as much as receiving. And he instinctively knew that the blonde didn't share that opinion.

Not to mention that his body didn't react like he expected it would when their eyes briefly met. There was no flash, no instant desire. Nothing beyond a bored expectation.

Now her friend...yeah, there had been some reaction there, reaction that caught him completely by surprise. Some of his blood had definitely rushed south when he met the pixie's eyes. Only he doubted she would appreciate being called a pixie, despite the deep red hair and porcelain skin and exquisite features.

And he seriously doubted she was the kind of one-night distraction he was looking for. Not that he really expected to find that distraction. Not here.

Which made him question again his decision to come here.

The bartender finally returned with his beer, pushing it in front of him before he sidled away, not even bothering to ask if he wanted to start a tab or pay on-the-go. Josh lifted the mug to his lips and took a long swallow, still watching the crowd from the corner of his eyes.

He had no idea why he was even bothering. He would finish this beer, pay the bartender and leave a generous tip, then go home and sleep for the next twenty hours.

Josh was half-way through the beer when he saw the pixie stand up and begin walking toward him—after some intense conversation with her friends. She hesitantly made her way to the bar, trying to squeeze through the crowd of noisy patrons. She was taller than he first thought, and not quite as fragile looking, but she still had a tough time making her way to the bar until Josh pointedly glared at the several people blocking her way. She finally pushed through the sudden opening, stepping close enough to rest her arms along the polished edge of the counter. The front of her loose-fitting shirt parted slightly when she crossed her arms, treating him to an appreciative view of the swell of her right breast and the barest glimpse of dark green lace.

More blood rushed south and he shifted just the smallest bit. She turned her head in his direction, briefly meeting his eyes before looking away, a hint of blush tingeing her cheeks. She looked up again and leaned slightly forward, her shirt opening even more as she tried to motion for the bartender. There was no doubt in Josh's mind that the move was purely accidental and completely lacking in motive, which made the forbidden glimpse even hotter.

And made him feel guilty as hell, like he was taking advantage of something he shouldn't.

He turned his head away and caught the bartender's eye, motioning him over then nodding at the woman. The guy immediately went over to her and asked for her order but she hesitated, and Josh felt her eyes on him. He looked over, once again meeting her bright hazel gaze and holding it as she offered him a shy smile.

"Thanks for getting his attention. Um, would you mind...I mean, would you like another drink? I could buy you another one." Her smile broadened even as the blush on her cheeks grew brighter, intriguing him further. He stepped closer to her, so close she had to tilt her head back to look up at him. But she didn't move away, didn't blink or flinch. Interesting.

He offered her a smile then shook his head. "No, thank you." Her smile faded and this time she did move to step back, but Josh reached out and gently cupped her elbow, keeping her in place. "But I'd love to buy you one. What would you like?"

"Oh. Um...I'm..." She paused and looked around, like she was trying to figure out what to do. He smiled again then turned toward the bartender.

"Another draft, and a white wine for the lady."

Her eyes widened in surprise, and Josh noticed the green and gold flecks in her irises. Emeralds and gold came to mind, and he shook his head at the fanciful thought, instead answering her unasked question. "I noticed what you were drinking when I walked in."

If she thought it unusual that someone would notice such a small detail in the space of a few seconds from several yards away, she didn't say so. From the way her eyes darted back and forth, and the slight way she fidgeted, Josh guessed she was still flustered. Probably from coming up and offering to buy him a drink. He got the feeling that wasn't something she did very often, if at all.

Which intrigued him even more.

He looked down, surprised to realize his hand was still cupping her elbow. He caressed the inside of her arm with his thumb, just a small movement. The flesh under his touch pebbled with goose bumps, and he noticed her slight shiver even as she tried to hide it. He gently released his hold and motioned to the empty stool next to her. She lifted herself into it and turned so she was half-facing the bar, and half-facing him. Josh took advantage of the position and stepped even closer, positioning himself between her legs.

"I'm Josh." He introduced himself, even holding out his hand. She placed her own hand in his and he folded his fingers around it, feeling the soft flesh and delicate bones under his touch. He squeezed gently but didn't let go, and offered her a small smile when she didn't try to pull away.

"I'm Shelby."

"Shelby. I like that name. It's nice to meet you."

Another blush fanned across her cheekbones and she looked down for a second, then back up. She was either exceptionally talented at playing innocent and coy, or this really was something she never did.

Josh would bet his next month's salary on the latter.

The bartender returned with their drinks and again walked away without saying a word. Josh made a mental note to come in later and have a talk with the guy, to let him know he wasn't the enemy.

Later.

For right now, he just wanted to focus on Shelby.

He watched as she reached for her wine glass with her left hand, her right still gently held in his. She took a tentative sip then lowered it, her tongue darting out and licking a drop from her lips. Josh's groin tightened in response, an instantaneous reaction to the sight of her tongue sweeping across her full lower lip.

Yet he was painfully aware of the silence between them, at the uneasiness hovering just below the surface of Shelby's demeanor. He cleared his throat while he tried to clear his mind of images of her tongue sweeping over his swollen cock.

"So what's a nice girl like you doing picking up strangers in a bar?" He meant it as a joke, as a way to break the ice and make her more comfortable. But he realized it was the worst thing to say as soon as the words left his mouth. His hand tightened around hers as she tried to pull away and he shifted even closer, trapping her leg between his. "I'm sorry. My sense of humor sucks."

"Oh. Uh, no, that's okay. You're right. I don't...I'm not...I mean, my friends and I..." Her voice faded away as she looked over his shoulder. He turned his head in that direction, and noticed her two friends watching them carefully. They quickly looked away, pretending to be preoccupied with their own conversation.

Josh turned back to Shelby, surprised at the look of misery on her face. He squeezed her hand then released it, but didn't step back as he offered her a smile. "So let me guess. The three of you had a bet and you lost, so you were the one who had to come and try to pick up the misfit, right?"

"What? No! Misfit? God, no. Chrissy was going to but I—" She clamped her mouth shut, looking horrified at her sudden enthusiastic outburst. Josh laughed at her reaction, his first genuine laugh in too long.

"I was joking. Again. I told you, my sense of humor sucks." He reached out and claimed her hand again, absently rubbing his thumb along the inside of her wrist, gratified to see her relax. "Two questions for you, Shelby."

She smiled and raised her brows at him, a warm

mix of humor and curiosity lighting her eyes. "Okay. What?"

"First: how about doing a shot with me?"

"Wow, that was a pretty tame question." Her face puckered in mock thought before she smiled and nodded. "Sure, I'll do a shot with you. What's your second question?"

"Hang on." Josh turned around and waved for the bartender, who warily made his way over again. He ordered the shots, then turned back to Shelby. Her head was tilted to the side, and she was studying the bartender with a curious gaze.

"He acts like he knows you, but he doesn't like you. I wonder why." Her voice was pitched low, almost a whisper, like she was thinking out loud. Josh would have missed hearing it completely if he hadn't been paying such close attention to her. She looked up at him, her eyes suddenly drifting back into focus, and she shook her head, laughing like she had been caught at something. "Sorry. I was talking to myself."

"Don't worry about it. And no, he doesn't know me. Not really. But you're right, he doesn't like me. Maybe one day I'll tell you the story." One day? What the hell was he thinking? There wasn't going to be a 'one day'. If he was lucky...which was a really big *if*...there *might* be one night. Tonight. But that was it. He had no time for a relationship, no room in his life for the complications a relationship would bring.

The bartender returned with the shots—two generous-sized colorful drinks with just enough sweetness to hide the alcohol. Josh yanked his wallet from his back pocket, careful not to open it all the way—Christ, the last thing he needed was to scare her off—and absently pulled several bills out and tossed them on the bar. The guy looked surprised, then reached down for the money and grudgingly nodded at Josh before walking away, his attitude noticeably less frigid. Josh ignored him, reaching out for the first glass and handing it to Shelby before picking up his own. He tapped his glass gently to hers, raised it in a small salute, then brought the glass to his lips and tossed it back in one swallow.

When he lowered his head, he noticed that Shelby was still studying the drink, her brow furrowed in concentration. She looked up, then made a small face when she noticed his drink was empty. She smiled, then slowly lifted the glass to her lips, taking a small sip then finally tossing it back. He watched her shudder just a bit, then stepped even closer when he saw that she was ready to lick her lips.

He leaned into her, taking a chance, offering no warning, asking no permission. He just claimed her mouth with his, a gentle meeting of the lips that he quickly deepened.

His tongue darted out and swept across her lips, tasting the left-over sweetness of the drink and the even sweeter taste of the woman herself. Her mouth opened in surprise and he wasted no time invading, sweeping his tongue inside her warmth, feeling her own tongue meet his in response. She sighed into his mouth, the sound a small whimper of surrender as she pressed her upper body against him, her hand fisting the material of his shirt. He wrapped one arm around her waist and pulled her even closer, feeling her soft curves as she molded herself to him.

He gentled the kiss and pulled away. No easy thing to do when she sighed in disappointment and leaned even closer against him. So close that it would be impossible for her not to feel the extent of his raging hard-on, not when he was standing between her legs like he was.

All that from a kiss. An all-too-brief and all-too-public kiss.

He cleared his throat and looked down at her, at the vixen disguised as a pixie. Because surely only a vixen could have this kind of heady effect on him. He was gratified to see that she had been just as affected. Her eyes fluttered open, a dazed expression in their deep emerald and gold depths. She blinked, a rapid sweeping of long dark lashes over porcelain skin, before her eyes widened in shock. She pulled back, her mouth forming a small O of surprise as her gaze darted around. He leaned forward and kissed her once more, a brief touching of lips, before she could say anything, before she had the chance to regret the public display.

"Second question: do you like motorcycles?"

"What?" She looked up at him and blinked again, like she was trying to focus. Josh briefly wondered if maybe the shot had been too much, or maybe she had more to drink earlier than he thought. Maybe she wasn't dazed from their kiss, maybe she was just intoxicated.

Which would be just his luck.

But no. She blinked one more time, her gaze clearing as she looked up at him. A flush blossomed on her face, and she looked a little surprised and embarrassed, but not intoxicated.

Thank you, Lord.

"Motorcycles. Um, yeah. I think. Maybe. I mean, I've never really been on one so I don't know, but they look like fun."

Josh closed his hand around hers and pulled her

from the stool, smiling when she pressed against him as she stood. "Then let's go find out."

Chapter Three

Shelby liked motorcycles. No, she amended, she loved motorcycles. She loved the sense of freedom, with the wind pulling at her hair as the night flew by around them, as the warmth of the summer air brushed across her skin.

Or maybe it was the man in front of her, who expertly maneuvered them through the streets. Her body was pressed tight against his, the heat of his back keeping her warm, the scent of worn leather and pure male as intoxicating as the shots they had shared at the bar.

She hadn't been sure what to do with her arms, didn't know where to put her hands when she first straddled the bike behind him. Josh had glanced over his shoulder at her, a smile in his eyes as if he sensed her uncertainty. He reached for her arms and draped them around his waist. They had sped down several blocks before he reached for her left hand and slid it down to rest on his thigh...dangerously high on his thigh.

That's when she learned that the denim of his jeans was as worn and soft as she first thought. And that his legs were as hard and muscular as she first thought. The man did not have an ounce of fat on him.

She still couldn't believe she had picked him up at the bar. Or maybe he was the one who had picked her up. It didn't matter, because she was here with him now, her body pressed against his as they sped through the city streets. As dangerous as this could be, she felt oddly safe with him. Safe, and comfortable. Odd that she should feel that way, so far out of her own self-imposed comfort zone.

Josh slowed the motorcycle to a near-stop and turned into the entrance of a small marina, maneuvering it to an empty parking space near the water. He cut the engine and they were immediately surrounded by the silence of the night, the occasional lap of water splashing against the bulkhead the only sound. Shelby closed her eyes and breathed in the scents of leather and man and harbor, thinking someone should bottle the smell for use in relaxation aroma therapy.

Josh's hand briefly tightened around hers before releasing it. He shifted, lowering the kick stand and dismounting from the motorcycle in one fluid move without Shelby even moving. She shifted on the seat and looked around, chewing on her lower lip as she wondered what to do next.

She didn't have time to think long, because Josh reached out and cupped her chin in his hand, turning her face toward his. Their eyes met, a brief heat firing between them before he lowered his mouth to hers in a slow languid kiss that curled her toes and left her clinging to him.

"I have a boat here, if you want to go have a drink." He paused, his eyes searching hers for a long second before he leaned back, putting some distance between them. "Or I can take you back to the bar if you want. Up to you."

His words surprised her—and touched her. Which was strange, considering this was supposed to be a one-night pick-up. Again she was impressed by how safe she felt with him, and she knew that, despite the air of danger surrounding him, he would do nothing to hurt her. Just like she knew that if she asked for him to take her back, he would, with no questions and no hesitation.

But she didn't want to go back. She wanted to go crazy. She wanted to taste the wilder side of life, just for tonight.

And she wanted to do it with this man.

Shelby looked up at him and smiled. "I think a drink sounds great."

Josh returned her smile, heat simmering in his dark eyes as he leaned forward and hauled her off the bike, holding her against him as he kissed her again. She tasted the hint of passion held in check and a shiver of anticipation raced through her, firing her blood and pooling between her legs. He grabbed her hand and led her across the parking lot to one of the piers. The sound of their footsteps against the wood echoed around them, the hollow sound swallowed by the dark water below.

Josh stopped in front of an older cabin cruiser, maybe 32-feet long, and dug into his front pocket, pulling out another set of keys. He released her hand and motioned for her to wait, then walked out onto the catwalk and climbed onboard. He unlocked the cabin door and disappeared inside for several minutes.

Shelby used the solitude to take several deep calming breaths. Her pulse had nearly steadied by the time he reappeared, minus the motorcycle jacket. And she had been right—his arms were as well-built as the rest of him, the sleeves of his polo stretched tight across his biceps. Shelby swallowed, her pulse quickening again as he offered her another smile and motioned her forward. She moved onto the catwalk then reached for his hand as she stepped across, landing on the deck with a soft thud and a stumble.

Right against his broad chest.

Her breath hitched as his arms came around her, holding her close. Their eyes met, and again fiery awareness sparked between them. But even as she swore he would kiss her again, Josh stepped back, putting distance between them. Shelby swallowed her disappointment as he absently waved around them.

"Welcome to *The Boat*. I haven't been out here in a couple of weeks so I wanted to go below and open everything up, make sure it wasn't too suffocating. Do you want the grand tour?"

"Oh. Um, yeah, sure." Shelby wasn't sure what the grand tour could encompass. Even from where she was standing on the back deck, she could tell there wasn't a lot of room below. But she quietly followed him, watching her step as he led her through the cabin door.

The back portion contained an elevated seat positioned in front of the wheel and an instrument panel that looked entirely too complicated to her. A stuffed upholstered bench seat stretched across the other side, comfortable looking despite its smaller size. A stereo and even a small television set were mounted across from the bench—or maybe it was a sofa, Shelby wasn't sure. Despite the instrument panel and small size, the area was cozy and inviting. She could imagine stretching out on the bench, relaxing or reading as he wheeled the boat out into the bay.

Like that was ever going to happen.

She shook the thought from her head and looked around, then followed Josh down the three steps that led further below, taking his hand for balance as she ducked her head. Here was the small galley area, compact and functional, and even a little fancier than she had expected. A dining area sat across from the galley, complete with two linen placemats and even a pillar candle centerpiece. The candle was recently lit, bathing the area with the soft light of a flickering flame.

Shelby glanced past Josh to the forward area, her eyes taking in the partially opened door which must lead to the main berth. She could see the corner of a raised bed, as well as more softly flickering light, and knew that he must have not only opened the windows and hatches, but lit several candles as well.

She didn't know whether to smile at the gesture, or to be more nervous about it. She was still deciding between the two when Josh brushed against her as he moved toward the small refrigerator in the galley.

"Sorry, there's not a lot of room here. I hope you weren't expecting a yacht."

"No, this is nice. Cozy."

"Is cozy another word for small?" He turned and offered her an opened bottle of beer, a lazy smile turning up the corners of his mouth. She pulled her gaze away from his face and took the beer from him, her fingers grazing his and sending a jolt up her arm. If he noticed, he didn't say anything. He just leaned against the counter and sipped from his own bottle, his eyes watching her.

"No, not small. Comfortable."

"Comfortable." He seemed to think about that, his eyes still focused on hers. "'Comfortable' is a good word. But I think I like 'intimate' better."

The air around her shifted, became hotter, closer. Shelby took a quick drink from the bottle, hoping the cold beer would lower her sudden fever. She didn't have a chance to find out, because Josh closed the distance between them and removed the bottle from her hand, reaching behind him and placing it in the small sink next to his.

And then she was in his arms, his mouth covering hers in a deep kiss that fed the hungry flames inside her. She pressed herself against him, needing to feel the hard edges and planes of his body against hers. He cupped her face in his hands and tilted her head back, devouring her mouth with his, demanding she open to his invasion. She gladly did, eagerly meeting his thrusting tongue, inviting him to explore as she did the same.

He lowered one hand, his fingers tracing the line of her neck and shoulder and lower, burning a trail across her flesh as he quickly undid the buttons of her shirt and pushed it down, pinning her arms to her sides with the material. He pulled his mouth from hers and looked down, pure male admiration shining in his dark eyes as he traced the lacy edges of her bra.

His palm skimmed across her covered nipple, teasing the hard peak, brushing back and forth until the friction of lace and skin became a sweet torment that a coaxed a groan from her parted lips. He lowered his other hand, a slow descent to her other breast for more sweet torture. Shelby shifted, craving the friction but needing more, so much more. She thrust her hips forward against his, rubbing herself against the hard outline of his erection.

Josh groaned and pressed his hips against her, hard and teasing, his breath hot on her skin as he dragged his mouth along her neck and down, down until he closed his mouth over one hardened nipple. Shelby's head fell back and the breath rushed from her lungs as he pulled the nipple into his mouth, licking and sucking, stoking the liquid fire that spread through her like lava.

His fingers trailed across her stomach, down to undo the button of her linen slacks and ease the zipper down. The back of his hand skimmed across the lace of her thong, teasing lightly as he pushed the pants down past her hips. They dropped with a whisper of material, pooling at her ankles as he ran his hand down one thigh and up the other, the roughened skin of his palm gentle against her heated flesh.

He pulled away, and the touch of a cool breeze replaced the hot moistness of his mouth against her hardened nipple, treating her to another sensual sensation. Shelby forced her eyes open and met his heated gaze, surprised by the passion and desire focused solely on her. His arms closed around her waist and he lifted her against him, turning and dislodging her loose clothing all at once, so that she was covered in nothing but her bra and thong and leather sandals.

He took one step and lifted her higher, then eased her down on the edge of the dinette table. Shelby reached out and grabbed his shoulders, afraid the table would collapse under her.

"Shh. Don't worry." The hoarse words came out just above a whisper, ragged and raw. Shelby loosened her grip on him, then dragged her own hands down along his shoulders and chest, grabbing his shirt and tugging.

"Someone here has on too many clothes." Her teasing words came out breathier than she planned, surprising her. She had never been one to talk much during foreplay or sex, had never been comfortable with teasing banter, but with him, here and now, it felt right.

She lowered her eyes and concentrated on pulling his shirt free from the waistband of his jeans, inching it up slowly as she glided the palms of her hands along the soft skin stretched tight over hard muscle. She pushed the material up higher, revealing his trim waist and sculpted abs, his broad chest and the dusting of dark hair that trailed down, narrowing until it disappeared into the waistband of his jeans.

She lost patience with her own slow strip tease and pushed the shirt the rest of the way up, until Josh reached down and yanked it over his head, revealing the top portion of a very delectable package. Shelby licked her lips and stared at him, running both of her hands over the expanse of skin and muscle. A small scar marred the smoothness of his chest just below his left shoulder, an oddly jagged line several inches long. But instead of distracting from the perfection of his body, it made him more appealing, more attainable, more human. It made him real, somehow.

And sexy as hell.

She dipped her head forward and lightly kissed the imperfection, trailing her lips along the line. His muscles quivered under her touch and she felt his chest hitch with a heavy breath. She smiled, feeling a sense of power in knowing that she could affect him the way he affected her.

Her hands continued trailing down, her nails gently grazing his ribs, his abdomen, following the thin line of hair that led even further down. She reached for the button of his jeans, quickly undoing it and his zipper before pushing both his jeans and his briefs past his hips.

The hard length of his erection sprang into her hand and she closed her fingers around the heated thickness, marveling at the contrasting feel of steel and satin. Her thumb brushed at the drop of wetness on the smooth tip as she stroked him, long glides up and down his throbbing shaft.

The height of the table was perfect and she slid the smallest bit forward, just enough that she could rub the tip of his cock against the damp lace of her thong. Heat exploded inside her at just that small contact, heat and a desire so raw, so new and foreign to her, that it took her breath away. And suddenly she wanted him, all of him, deep inside her. She wanted to feel his hard length diving into her, needed to wrap her legs around his waist and close herself over him, milking him.

A small groan made her look up but she barely had time to register the smoldering look in Josh's eyes before he crushed his mouth against hers. This was no longer passion restrained; instead it was a conquering—of her mind, of her senses, of her body.

She willingly surrendered, her hands roaming over his body, seeking, searching, as his mouth devoured hers. More heat pooled inside her and gathered into a liquid fire between her legs.

Josh pulled away, said something that didn't make

sense until he leaned behind her and blew out the candle. His arm swept to the side and she heard the muted sound of glass cracking but she didn't care because he pushed her back on the table, her ass hanging just over the edge, her legs dangling down. Josh leaned over her, one arm braced along her side as he folded his hand around his cock and rubbed the hard tip against her covered opening.

It was too much, the teasing, yet not enough. She wanted to feel him there, but inside as well. Shelby ran the fingers of her right hand down along her own neck, skimming, lightly touching her breast and stomach, loving how his eyes darkened as he watched the progress of her hand.

Tonight was about being wild, about living life, about experiences yet to be discovered. Just tonight. So she brought her hand up again to her breast, touching herself through the lace before sliding the thin material down to bare herself to his heated gaze. Her fingers closed around her nipple, squeezing and tugging. A swirl of feeling tightened inside her and she arched her back, surprised at the pull she felt deep inside her.

She moved her hand from her breast and splayed her fingers against her skin, sliding them down, reveling in the look in his eyes, at the power and freedom unleashed by that look. She slid her fingers lower, across the front of her thong, tangling in his, teasing the tip of his cock and drawing a sharp breath from him as she pulled the lace covering to the side, opening herself to his gaze. To him.

Josh pushed away from the table, straightening long enough to push his pants down and off before he stepped even closer to her. He reached out with both hands, holding her thong further to the side as he slid one finger along her wet clit then inside her. Her back arched and she thrust her hips forward, urging him deeper, needing more.

"Don't stop touching yourself." Her raspy words surprised her, as much as the boldness of her own touch against her clit surprised her. Josh offered her a rakish smile that sent tendrils of excitement through her entire body as he let go of her thong and again closed his hand around his thick length, stroking himself with long, slow movements against her moist heat.

He eased his finger slowly out of her, then slid two fingers back inside, matching the rhythm of the slow strokes against his cock. More. She wanted more.

She spread her legs further apart and discovered that she could rest her feet on the seats on either side of the table. She braced her heels on both benches and slid just the tiniest bit forward, opening herself even further to his touch and gaze. Yet it still wasn't enough. She had barely tasted the wildness growing inside her; now she wanted it all.

She reached down again and pulled her thong all the way to the side, holding it there as she rubbed her clit with one finger, back and forth, the friction of her touch igniting flames deep inside her. Josh slid his fingers out then dragged them up her lips, using her own wetness to lubricate her even more before plunging his fingers deep inside. The friction, the rhythm, the sensation of touch inside and out built together, swirling in a ribbon of excitement, coming together and separating, coming together again. The pressure continued building, growing, pushing her to a steep ledge she had never seen before, not like this.

And she wanted nothing more than to be pushed

off that ledge.

Her back arched and she thrust her hips closer to Josh, impaling herself more fully on his fingers, already deep inside her. He moved his hand, a slight twist of his wrist, and catapulted her over the edge. Her head fell back as wave after wave of sensation crashed over her, knocking her senseless before sending her to a height she never knew existed. Her body clenched around his hand, seeking more even as the tremors grew.

Josh moved away and she moaned at his loss, vaguely aware of him reaching for something, vaguely realizing he was unrolling a condom down his long shaft. Her hips thrust forward again, still searching as the tremors eased, fading into smaller aftershocks that gave her a chance to breathe.

Gave her a chance to think about what she had just done.

Guilt gnawed at the edges of her awareness; guilt, and something she was very much afraid was shame. She tried to push the feelings and thoughts away, refusing to let this night—this experience—be spoiled by some deep-seated antiquated notion of propriety.

Josh must have sensed a change in her, because he leaned over her and gently clasped her face in both of his hands. His eyes searched hers, dark and knowing, before he gave her his rakish smile and shook his head.

"You're not finished yet, sweetheart. You haven't even started." His mouth closed on hers, his tongue sweeping deep inside and chasing all thought away as the head of his cock pushed against her wet opening. A shudder racked her at the sensation of him being so close, but just as she was certain he would plunge deep inside her, he broke the kiss and pulled away.

But only far enough that he could kiss his way down her body, his mouth and tongue lavishing attention to her bare skin. His merest touch sent excitement soaring through her once more. His mouth closed over her dampness and his tongue raked against her clit and dove inside, stroking the fires that had only dampened, not gone out. And this time, when the explosion rocked her from inside out, when she didn't think she could survive without him anymore, he plunged inside her, burying himself so deep she felt him knocking at the edge of her soul.

And she had the briefest thought that should she ever open that door to him, she would be doomed.

And then she thought no more, just lost herself in his touch, giving herself up to every new move he taught her, giving in to every new sensation he coaxed from her.

Chapter Four

Josh was in a foul mood, a mood that had only disintegrated during the last forty-eight hours. He made no attempt to hide it as he strode through the cracked hallways of the precinct to the back section that housed the closet that passed for his office. He brushed by the other officers, some in uniform, some dressed in street clothes much as he was. It didn't matter, he ignored them all.

"Sgt. Nichols." He heard his name called behind him but he didn't bother to break stride. If it was important, whoever it was would keep calling him or chase after him or track him down in his office. Even if it wasn't important, they would track him down.

Which is what he should have done forty-eight hours—he glanced down at his watch and shook his head. Correction, fifty-three hours—ago. At precisely 3:59 Saturday morning when he woke in the front berth of his boat.

Alone.

He muttered a string of curses and shoved open

the door of his office, banging it against the dilapidated filing cabinet that was wedged in the corner. He ignored the swinging door and stepped around the boxes surrounding his desk before tossing his jacket across the back of his chair. His eyes shot to the phone, looking for the tell-tale blinking light that would indicate he had messages waiting.

And of course he did. But he knew none of them were from *her*.

From Shelby.

Because she didn't know who he was. She didn't know his last name, had no idea where he lived or where he worked.

Just like he didn't know anything about her. He hadn't thought to ask for anything other than her first name at the beginning of the night, thinking the entire encounter was just a very lucky one-night thing. Then, when he realized he most definitely wanted more than just one night, that he was definitely interested in seeing her again, they were both otherwise preoccupied.

Yeah, asking a woman for her phone number when she was on her knees in front of you, with your cock so deep in her throat you thought you were on your way to heaven, just struck him as shitty timing.

If he had known then that she was going to skip out on him, just up and disappear, he would have asked her for her damn phone number, no matter what they had been doing.

Shit. He hadn't figured her for a runner. He also hadn't figured her for a wild vixen, but she was. His cock twitched in memory of their untamed hours together, even as his inner gut assured him that Friday night was a first for her. It had to have been. Her emotions, her reactions, her responses were too genuine, too real and amazingly, irresistibly, mind-blowing honest to be an act.

No, she most definitely hadn't been a virgin. But he was almost positive she wasn't very experienced, either.

Josh shifted then grunted as he glanced through the stack of papers that had piled on the edge of his desk. Yeah, he told himself, he was *almost* positive. Like he had been *almost* positive that she was going to wake up in his arms Saturday morning.

"Sgt. Nichols!"

"What?" Josh bellowed, not bothering to hide his impatience at being tracked down within minutes of showing up. The cadet that appeared in his doorway flinched, a look of apprehension on his freshly scrubbed face. Josh figured the kid was barely old enough to shave, let alone become a police officer. Baltimore must be getting desperate to be hiring them so young.

"Sgt. Nichols, I'm sorry, but the lieutenant wants to see you. Right away, he said."

Josh waved his hand at the cadet, acknowledging and dismissing him with one motion. He couldn't begin to guess what the lieutenant might want with him and didn't bother to try. He grabbed the heavy duty radio from its charger and walked out of his office, heading back the way he came.

The lieutenant's office was upstairs, tucked back into a corner that pretty much guaranteed privacy and peace and quiet. Not that he was there often enough to enjoy the advantages, but Josh knew it came in handy for some meetings. Like when he wanted to talk 'off-the-record'...or chew someone out. Josh wondered what this one would be as he climbed the steps and stopped outside the open door, rapping on the frame with his knuckles.

"Josh, come on in, have a seat." The lieutenant didn't bother to stand as he motioned him forward and Josh took both that and the fact that he called him by his first name as good signs. He sank into the ancient chair, hearing it squeak under his weight as he shifted and tried to get comfortable.

"Good work this week. You and your team have done a fantastic job. The numbers are looking really good."

"Thank you, sir."

The lieutenant leaned back in his own chair and steepled his fingers under his chin, fixing Josh with a steady look. "Which is why I hate to do this, but I need to reassign you. Temporarily, only. A week, if that long."

"Sir?"

"There's been a disturbance of some kind at the Historical Society. Vandalism and theft. I need you to work on it."

Josh shifted in the chair again, barely restraining himself from jumping out of it in irritation. "I'm not sure I understand, sir. What does that have to do with vice?"

"Absolutely nothing. But this case is a sensitive one and I was asked to put my best guy on it. That means you."

"Thank you sir, but I still don't understand."

"It seems that there were certain artifacts on loan, artifacts that were being restored and studied before being put on display for a special exhibit. The artifacts are on loan from the National Park Service, which means this is now a Federal case."

"Which means the FBI would be involved, not us."

"The FBI, the Department of the Interior and Homeland Security."

Josh straightened at that news. He had never heard of all three agencies working together on something like this. "Now I really don't understand. Why would such a mix of alphabet soup be involved in something as simple as vandalism and theft?"

"It's not exactly 'simple'. Apparently, when one of the artifacts missing is a lock of Presidential hair, something like petty theft and vandalism becomes very political."

"Excuse me?" Josh didn't think he had heard correctly. Or maybe he had, and this was the lieutenant's idea of a joke. A really bad joke.

But no, the expression on the lieutenant's face was dead serious. Josh leaned back in the chair and met the man's eyes, trying to read his mind and failing. The lieutenant was obviously much more gifted in that area, because he pushed a file across the desk toward Josh and offered him an apologetic smile.

"Congratulations, Sergeant. Until the artifacts are located and this great crime of the century is solved, you've been promoted to Babysitter. Now go make sure the boys all play nice and actually solve the crime instead of fighting each other in our sandbox."

Josh stared down at the folder, still not believing it. From Vice Squad Team Leader to Babysitter. He stood and grabbed the folder then walked out of the room, wondering who he had cosmically pissed off so much that his life had taken such a drastic spiral into hell over the last few days.

Chapter Five

Shelby wanted her space back. No, she wanted more than her space back—she wanted peace and quiet. She wanted to be left alone. She wanted a do-over from Sunday night on.

Memories of her wild encounter Friday night came vividly to mind, sending heat through her body and, she was certain, across her cheeks. Maybe she needed a do-over from Friday night on, because surely this was some weird karmic payback sent down on her by the Fates.

And this really wasn't the time for her to be remembering everything that happened Friday night. It really wasn't, not with everything else falling apart around her.

She finally noticed the silence in the room and looked up to see four sets of eyes focused on her, studying her. None of them were sympathetic. One set in particular was actually accusing—her supervisor, David Spear. Her ex-fiancé. And probably soon-to-be ex-supervisor, as well.

She swallowed against the dryness that threatened to close her throat. Shelby had done nothing wrong—not about this—but the constant barrage of questions and silent stares filled her with guilt.

"May I have some water please?" Her voice cracked from lack of use, and probably from nerves as well. For all the questions that had been thrown her way, she hadn't really been given a chance to answer them. Well, that wasn't quite true. She answered them the first two times they had been asked. It was the other dozen times that her attempts at answering had been walked over.

Her request was ignored, all four men acting like she hadn't spoken at all. And suddenly it was too much. *She* was not the guilty party here, and she was tired of being treated like a criminal in her own office.

Shelby took a deep breath and straightened, trying to channel some of the bravado and self-confidence that had filled her Friday night. "Gentlemen, is anyone actually doing anything to locate the artifacts? Or is everyone simply content to stand here and stare me down like I'm a common criminal?"

One of the men leaned across the table and fixed her with an intimidating stare. Shelby thought he was from the Department of the Interior but couldn't remember, since they all happened to be dressed the same. "Ms. Martin, I don't think you realize the seriousness of this situation. The artifacts are federal property and they were in your care. You were the last person to see them."

"No sir. The last person to see them was the person who stole them. *I* saw them Friday evening, when I properly locked them up and secured them before leaving. And I *do* happen to understand the seriousness. More than any of you here, sir, I understand and appreciate exactly how valuable those artifacts are. And I do not mean valuable in a monetary way. The historical importance far outweighs—"

"Shelby, enough. These gentlemen are only doing their jobs." David interrupted her, his words immediately deflating her confidence. Her shoulders slumped and she stared down at her hands, properly folded on the table in front of her. He opened his mouth to say something else, but stopped when the door opened behind him.

Shelby was almost thankful for that, until she noticed the local police officer peer inside and look around as if trying to figure out who was in charge. His eyes finally settled on the older gentleman across from her, the one who had done most of the questioning. "Sgt. Nichols is here. He'll be acting as liaison for this case."

The door opened wider, admitting the new arrival. Shelby's surprise at hearing there would be yet one more person to interrogate her disappeared when she raised her head and saw the newcomer. Her mouth dropped open in shock and the small squeak that filled the room had come from her. She snapped her mouth shut and tried to look away, but his gaze locked on hers and held it.

This really was karmic payback from the Fates, because it was *him*. Josh. Her wild, once-in-a-lifetime fantasy encounter. He looked even better than she remembered. And so out of place in this room full of stuffy suits in his jeans and polo shirt.

He was a police officer? But he couldn't be! Yet there was his badge, clipped to the waistband of his worn denim jeans, along with a very lethal and intimidating gun. Oh my God. The Fates really were punishing her for her uncharacteristic behavior Friday night. That was the only possible explanation for how things had gone so wrong in such a short period of time.

He entered the room, his presence quickly filling the small space and overshadowing everyone else. His eyes stayed locked on hers but he gave her no sign of recognition. Although Shelby figured there was probably a good chance that the slight twitch in his clenched jaw might have something to do with her.

Shelby pulled her gaze away from his and stared down at her folded hands as introductions were made. She sensed additional tension in the room and instinctively knew it wasn't just from seeing him again. This tension was more masculine, like a pack of dogs fighting for the top alpha spot.

One of the suited men gave a brief explanation of the situation—entirely too brief, considering she had been kept cooped up in this stuffy room for a couple of hours, being asked the same questions over and over.

Josh—Sgt. Nichols—nodded at the end of the explanation then focused his attention on her. His dark gaze was professionally neutral and Shelby wondered what he was thinking. Then she decided she probably didn't want to know.

"And this lady is...?"

"Dr. Shelby Martin. She's our lead archivist and conservator, and the last one who saw the stolen artifacts." Shelby ground her teeth at the condescending accusation in David's voice but said nothing, just looked straight ahead, focusing her stare on the door as she entertained thoughts of making a mad dash for freedom.

"*Dr. Martin*. I see. And when did *Dr. Martin* last see the artifacts?"

"When I secured them Friday before leaving for the evening." Shelby felt the heat spread across her cheeks but she refused to look over at Josh. She knew he was watching her, could feel her skin tingle everywhere his eyes touched, but she couldn't look at him.

"Who discovered them missing? And when?"

"Our custodial team noticed the damage last night and alerted me."

"Last night? Is the custodial team here every night?"

"Yes, of course."

"Nothing out of the ordinary reported between Friday night and last night?"

"No, of course not. We would have reported it immediately." David straightened, as if the question insulted his integrity.

"Video surveillance?"

And now it was David's turn to squirm, something Shelby secretly relished as she waited for his answer. "Um, unfortunately, no. Our, um, system seems to have erased, uh, footage from this, um, weekend."

"I see."

Shelby finally looked over at Josh and saw him taking notes. He made a few final scratches on the small pad then tucked it into his back pocket and turned his attention to the three federal suits. "Well, gentlemen, I have all the information I need. I'm only acting as liaison here, so if there's anything you need from our department, please let me know." He handed business cards to the three men and turned toward the door then paused. "I do have one question, though. Is Miss—excuse me—*Doctor* Martin a suspect?"

There was some foot shuffling and muttering before one of the men straightened. "Of course not, no. As of right now, we don't believe she has any involvement in this."

Shelby's mouth dropped open. No involvement? If they thought that, then why had she been kept here and made to endure their incessant questions?

"Interesting. I know you guys tend to do things a little differently, but do you mind if I ask why she looks like she's been detained and interrogated?"

More shuffling and throat-clearing occurred before the same gentleman answered. "Dr. Spear was adamant that she might be able to offer some insight, as she was the last person to see them."

"And she's in charge of them. It's *her* responsibility if anything happens to them!" David added quickly. Shelby turned to look at him through narrowed eyes, wishing that looks could kill. If they did, his smarmy body would be writhing on the ground in agony right now.

"In that case, if you gentlemen don't mind, I believe I'll escort Dr. Martin out. I may have a few questions for her myself, and I'd be interested in getting her...insight." He nodded to the gentlemen then turned his gaze on Shelby.

And suddenly, this suffocating room seemed to be the safest place for her.

Because his gaze wasn't completely blank, not anymore. When he looked at her, she saw a flash in his dark eyes, and that flash did not bode well for her. It wasn't the flash of passion or desire that she had seen Friday night. This was a flash of anger, and something else she couldn't quite make out. All she knew was that she did not want to leave, not with him.

But he stood there, holding the door open with one large hand, waiting for her. And she knew she didn't have a valid excuse for not going, not one that she could voice. So she took a deep breath and stood, taking an extra long minute to straighten her skirt and blouse before lifting her chin high and strolling past him as if she didn't have a care in the world.

Chapter Six

Josh almost smiled. Almost. His mood hadn't yet improved that much. But seeing his Friday night vixen marching so regally in front of him was helping. It wasn't her stiff and regal manner, though—it was the unusually fast pace she was setting, like she wanted to run but knew she couldn't.

Yeah, she definitely knew that he was not a happy person right now.

She made a sudden turn down a hallway that led deeper into the building and Josh picked up his own pace, catching up to her and grabbing her elbow. "Where do you think you're going?"

She stopped, surprise etched across her face as she looked down at his hand. He ran his thumb across the soft skin, just to see what she would do. Sure enough, she yanked her arm free, but not before he saw her flesh pebble at his touch. He bit back his smile, giving her a stern look that made her take a hesitant step back. The heel of her sensible flats caught in the hem of her ridiculously long skirt, causing her to stumble. Josh reached for her arm to steady her but she caught herself and straightened. She lifted her chin a notch and glared over his shoulder, not meeting his eyes.

"I'm sorry, Sergeant, but I need to go to my office."

"Your office?"

"Yes. There are some things I need to get and I...that is..." Her voice drifted off as her chin dropped.

"Yes?"

"I need to use...there's something I need to do, that's all."

Josh figured her sudden discomfort had a lot more to do with something other than just his presence, and he studied her for a long minute before realization smacked him upside the head. "You need to use the bathroom."

Her cheeks flamed red as she nodded, still looking anywhere but at him. The regal bravado of a few minutes ago was gone, and Josh noticed how truly miserable she looked. "How long were in there with them?"

"I beg your pardon?"

"The Alphabet Soup Group. How long were you in there with them?"

"Oh. I'm not sure." She glanced down at her watch, her forehead creasing as she muttered to herself. "Since a little after seven o'clock this morning, right after I got here, after David called."

Almost three hours? Josh clenched his jaw as disbelief and anger surged through him. What possible excuse did they use to keep her confined in that small room for so long? For all the public negativity and scorn they usually received, Josh normally had respect for the Feds. Maybe they were a bit more stringent than suited him, but they were generally efficient straight-shooters. He had been able to tell within the first five minutes that the woman in front of him had nothing to do with the theft. Surely the Alphabet Soup Group had been able to figure the same thing out.

Josh said nothing, though, and motioned her forward. He made a mental note to look into things a bit more on his own. As liaison, he was officially on day-duty until no longer needed. Unless the boys refused to play nice with each other, that meant his days would be filled with catching up on paperwork. He'd have plenty of time to do a little unofficial investigation.

Josh followed her into a cluttered office, watching as she hurried to a door on the far side. The bathroom, no doubt. The door clicked shut with a bang, and Josh no longer bothered to hide his smile.

His Friday night vixen was a doctor. Of all things. He would have never guessed that one. Of course, he hadn't given her occupation much thought, not when there was so much more to keep him—keep both of them—preoccupied.

He wasted the several minutes waiting for her by looking around her office, taking in the cluttered desk, the frames and pictures hanging from the wall, the collections of old things scattered haphazardly on various shelves throughout the room. His mouth tilted in a small grin when he noticed the silly Felix the Cat clock hanging on the wall, its tail swinging back and forth with each second.

Apparently his little vixen had a taste for vintage memorabilia.

Josh glanced around the room, taking in everything once more but without really seeing them.

No, in his mind's eye, he saw Shelby, stretched across the dinette of his boat, her hands shyly touching herself.

Shelby, with her thick red hair spread across his chest and waist as she took him in her mouth.

Shelby, with her head tossed back, her perfect breasts jutting forward as she straddled him, riding him until her body shook with her release.

Shit.

Josh reached down and adjusted his semi-hard cock, thinking he'd be better off remembering *anything* but Friday night. Except that wasn't going to be easy to do, not when he decided he wanted a repeat. And another. And another.

His little vixen may have only counted on one wild night, but she was going to get much more than that. Especially now that he knew who she was and where to find her. His anger at her just up and disappearing returned, putting a scowl on his face just as Shelby walked out of the bathroom. She stumbled to a stop and stared at him, her hand coming to rest on her chest, like she was startled. He watched as she took a hesitant step then stopped again, her eyes darting around the room. Josh would bet his next paycheck she was trying to figure out how to escape from him.

Again.

"Are you ready?"

"For what?"

Josh drew in a deep breath, held it, then let it out slowly. In the last ten minutes, he witnessed the woman in front of him go from hapless victim to regal doctor to fragile woman to absent-minded professor. And let's not forget adventurous vixen. He wondered which personality was the real Shelby Martin, and decided to make it his mission to find out.

But first he needed to get her out of here, because there were other things he wanted to find out first.

"Are you ready to come with me?" And damn, he hadn't meant for the words to come out like that, almost verbatim to phrases they had uttered to each other Friday night. So he ignored her flustered blush and plunged ahead. "I need to ask you some questions."

"Oh. Yes, I'm ready. I just need to grab my bag." She walked over to her desk and pulled open a drawer, removing a large handbag that she tossed over her shoulder. Then she bent down and grabbed an even bigger oversize tote bag from the floor and flung it over the same shoulder. Josh was surprised her shoulder didn't dislocate from all the weight.

She pushed past him and stepped into the hall, then waited for him to join her before she closed the door and carefully locked it. Without giving him so much as a glance, she started back up the hallway, her head held high as they exited the building. She paused, finally looking over at him, and Josh motioned to his car parked along the curb. Her shoulders slumped but she said nothing, just descended the steps and made her way to the unmarked sedan, stopping at the rear passenger door. He caught up to her, gave her an amused look, then reached around and opened the front door for her.

She looked down at the car, then up at him, confusion marring her porcelain features. "I'm not under arrest?"

Josh blinked, her absurd question catching him off-guard. But he kept a straight face and shook his head. "The last time I checked, it wasn't a crime to skip out on your partner after having the wildest, most adventurous, best damn sex of the century so no, *doctor*, you're not under arrest."

Her eyes widened and her mouth formed a small O of shock as a flush spread across her face. Then she shook her head and raised that stubborn chin again. "I'm sorry, *Sergeant*, but this weekend has been filled with many new experiences and I'm not quite sure how to react to any of them."

She lowered herself into the car and placed the bags between her feet, then reached around and pulled the seat belt across her chest, not bothering to look at him once. He closed the door and walked around to the other side, making sure she couldn't see him before he let his smile break free.

"That makes two of us, sweetheart. That definitely makes two of us."

Chapter Seven

Music drifted around her, filling every space of the empty room. She took a sip of the chilled wine, closed her eyes, and breathed in deeply. Through her nose and out her mouth. Another deep breath, through her nose and out her mouth.

Shelby opened her eyes and sighed, took a large swallow of the wine this time, then reached for the remote and clicked the stereo off. She glanced around, her eyes falling on the romance novel on the coffee table. She grabbed it and settled back, planning on losing herself in the love story.

But two chapters in, she stopped reading and tossed the book down, unable to get into the story. Instead of losing herself in the hero's glittering blue eyes, she was recalling a dark heated gaze. Instead of being wooed by a designer Armani suit, she craved the feel of soft denim and warm leather.

"Crazy. Absolutely insane." Her muttered words echoed around her and she shook her head. The past five days had completely turned her mundane world upside down, and she didn't know how to change it back.

She didn't know if she *wanted* to change it back. At least, not all of it. The theft and accusation of being a criminal was something she could do without, even if it wasn't really an accusation.

Allegedly.

She added that word to her list of most-hated words. *Allegedly*. What a stupid word anyway. It was just a fancy way of pointing a verbal finger and calling someone a liar or thief without proof. The "alleged" crime, the "alleged" accusations. Please.

It didn't help that Amanda and Chrissy both thought she was worrying over nothing. They hadn't been there, hadn't seen the coldness in David's eyes when he told those investigators she had been the last one with the artifacts. If she didn't know better, she would have thought he was actually enjoying it!

She frowned as she pictured David's face. His eyes had been glittering slits of triumph, his pale lips pressed in a tight line that pinched his face. A tight line of disapproval, or something else? Because even now, a week later, she couldn't shake the feeling that those tightly pressed lips had been his way of suppressing a smile. But why would he be smiling? David never smiled. Not at her, at least, not for a long time. He seriously couldn't be thinking she had anything to do with the theft. Could he?

And why was she so worried over what that slimy weasel thought, anyway?

Because he could have her fired, that was why. Or stop her promotion.

A shudder swept through her at the thought. No, he wouldn't do anything like that. They may not have parted on the best of terms but even he wouldn't stop so low.

At least those three investigators didn't seem to think she was guilty. She didn't think they did, anyway. If they had, wouldn't they have kept her even longer? Or thrown her in jail or come searching her apartment or something?

That's why her friends thought she had nothing to worry about.

Of course, she hadn't told them that her one-night stand had shown up and rescued her from more questions.

Well, maybe 'rescued' wasn't the right word, but he had gotten her out of that room.

Josh was a cop. How could he be a cop? But she should have known better, should have known that she couldn't pick someone up in a bar for a one-night stand and not have the experience come back and bite her on her tush. That's what she got for trying to be adventurous and wild and wanting something different, something she couldn't have.

She wasn't cut out for adventurous and wild and different.

But at least she hadn't told Amanda and Chrissy that. They had pushed her for details when they picked her up outside the marina that night, but she hadn't told them anything except that she had had fun. She was certain the dreamy smile on her face said so much more, but they hadn't pushed her.

Well, Amanda hadn't pushed her, and had stopped Chrissy when she would have continued the interrogation.

Which brought her mind straight back to Josh, and the fact that her one-night stand was a cop.

Shelby pushed herself up from the sofa and walked into the kitchen, thinking a cup of hot tea might soothe her rattled nerves. Of course, her mind continued to wander as she waited for the water to heat and no matter how hard she tried not to, all she could think about was one rugged, dangerous police officer.

Sergeant Josh Nichols.

She closed her eyes and shuddered. Her wild one-night-stand *would* be with a police officer. Of course it would. And for planning on never seeing him again—because really, what were the chances she would ever run into him again considering she hardly went out and he didn't seem the scholarly type anyway—well, that plan certainly hadn't worked. Of course, how could she have known someone would actually break in and steal artifacts? And that she would be held responsible for them?

And oh God, she could lose her job if they weren't recovered. David had made that quite clear. Even though she was innocent and had nothing to do with it...

The microwave timer dinged and Shelby pulled the steaming mug of water out, then tossed in a tea bag and dunked it several times, watching the water turn a dark shade. Almost like Josh's eyes...

"For crying out loud," she muttered. She put the mug on the counter and opened several cabinets, finally locating a bottle of brandy at the back of one shelf. She opened the bottle and poured a generous splash into the tea then took a sip.

There. Much better.

She walked back into the living room and eased down onto the sofa, curling her legs under her, cradling the mug with both hands as she stared down at the steaming liquid. No, the color of Josh's eyes was nothing like this. They were darker, almost like melted chocolate and...

Shelby shook her head in disgust. She was hopeless. It didn't help that she kept remembering his comment outside her office the other day, either. The wildest, most adventurous, best damn sex of the century. She snorted. Like she really believed that. For her, maybe. But she seriously doubted that was the case for him.

She wasn't quite sure where he had planned on taking her the other day. He had simply started driving, his hands clenching the steering wheel as often as he clenched his jaw. Several times he had looked over at her, and his mouth opened like he wanted to say something, but each time he snapped it shut and shook his head.

He did ask her about the artifacts, though. Just several simple questions that resulted in her explaining, in great detail, what each one was and why they were historically important. And not really worth much monetarily. Sure, there was still extended interest in the Civil War because of the big anniversary that had recently ended, but the artifacts still wouldn't bring in a lot of money.

Her long-winded explanation had been interrupted by his cell phone ringing, and then he had dropped her off at her car minutes later. He told her he'd be in touch, his dark gaze intent and focused on her, then he drove away.

"Melted chocolate. Definitely," she murmured, thinking of his eyes locked on hers. She took another sip of the tea and leaned her head against the back cushion, closing her eyes as she tried to relax. She'd finish this then go to bed.

The doorbell rang, startling her enough that she splashed tea on her bare leg. Muttering a curse, she wiped at the hot liquid with her hand, trying to cool it off as she stood and hopped to the kitchen to grab a wet paper towel. The bell rang again, longer this time. Whoever was out there was insistent.

Shelby finished dabbing at her leg, glad that the burn didn't show signs of blistering. She'd take a pinch from her aloe plant and put some on, as soon as she got rid of whoever was at the door.

The doorbell rang yet again, a constant buzzing as the button was held down. Shelby muttered another curse and stalked into the living room, prepared to read the riot act to whoever was on the other side. She yanked it open—

And came face-to-face with Sgt. Josh Nichols.

Chapter Eight

She must be seeing things. It couldn't really be him, could it?

Yes, it really was him. Josh was standing right there in front of her. Shelby stared at him for a brief second, leaning so casually against the door frame with a rakish smile on his face. His eyes drifted over her body, from her messy pony tail, to her oversized t-shirt and too-short cut-off sweatpants, to her bare feet and back up.

Definitely melted chocolate, she thought as she met his eyes.

Then she slammed the door shut in his face.

"You do know I'm armed, right? And that I'm authorized to use excessive force to gain entry?" His voice was only slightly muffled by the door, and held a hint of laughter. She frowned, wondering if it would be safer to just ignore him. But he pressed the doorbell again and buzzing filled her ears. "Does this thing work? Because I can stand out here all night testing it for you."

Shelby gritted her teeth and counted to three, then pasted a fake smile on her face and opened the door—but just enough that she could peer around the edge to look at him. "Sergeant Nichols. Is this an official visit?"

Laughter danced in his eyes, as if he knew he had caught her off-guard. His eyes raked over her again, igniting tiny fires along her skin, and he shrugged. "Would an official visit involve a strip search? Because if you say yes, then yeah, this is definitely an official visit."

Shelby's mouth dropped open in surprise at his bluntness, ignoring the instant desire that curled deep in her belly and lower. The man knew exactly what he was doing to her, dammit. And he really must be a mind reader because he pushed his way past her just as she was about to slam the door shut on him again. He stepped further into the living room, looking around and taking everything in with one long glance before he turned to face her.

Then he stepped toward her, pinning her between the now-closed door and his hard body. He caught her face between his hands and lowered his mouth to hers in a kiss that demanded her surrender. And damn her body, because it immediately obeyed him even as her mind screamed to push him away.

Instead she melted against him, her hands gripping his shoulders as her hips searched out his, seeking his hard length, searching for completion. His tongue swept inside her, teasing, coaxing a response from her as his hands slid down her sides to the hem of her shirt. He bunched the material in his fists and dragged it upwards. His callused palms slowly grazed the sensitive flesh of her stomach, her sides, each rib, slowly inching upward until he skimmed the underside of each breast. He reached around, dragging his hands closer together, and flipped a thumb across each nipple, teasing them to tight peaks.

Shelby dug her hands deeper into his shoulders, searching for support as he dragged his mouth from hers and along her jaw, down across her neck and back up to her ear. He nibbled on the sensitive ear lobe, then pulled it gently between his teeth, his breath hot against her flesh, intoxicating.

"Why did you leave the other night?"

"Hm?"

He nibbled the sensitive spot just under her ear, his teeth grazing the corded line of her neck before he whispered to her once more. "The other night. Tell me why you left."

"Hm?" He eased away from her, just an inch, just enough to put the tiniest distance between them. He lowered her shirt and placed his hands on either side of her face, forcing her to look at him as his words sunk in. His eyes held hers, serious and intent, as he repeated the demand one more time.

"Tell me why you left."

Shelby tried to look away as her mind searched for an answer, but he cupped her chin in one hand and turned her head, capturing her with his gentle hold and his steady gaze. His eyes demanded an answer and her mind could come up with nothing but the truth.

"I was afraid to stay."

"Why?"

She closed her eyes and shook her head, not wanting to answer. She felt his lips against hers, gentle and coaxing. "Tell me Shelby. Why were you afraid to stay?"

"Because..." She looked down, watched the steady

beat of the pulse in his throat, and licked her lips. Her eyes darted back up to meet his then looked away once more. "Because it was supposed to be just one night. One wild night of living life. I was afraid if I stayed, I'd want it to be more."

Josh lowered his head, leaning forward enough to capture her gaze with his own steady one. The unmasked desire she saw in their dark depths filled her with liquid heat. And with trepidation. She was too afraid that she could easily fall for this man, for his dangerous heat, for the dangerous passion he ignited within her. Afraid she could easily fall for an experience that was so far out of her comfort zone.

And she knew the end result would be catastrophic.

"Do you want me to leave?" The soft question, spoken in such a gentle tone, undid her. She should say yes. Every rational brain cell she possessed screamed at her to say yes. But she shook her head.

Should he leave? Oh yes, if she was to have any sanity remain in her world, he should leave. She should push him out the door and barricade herself inside. But she didn't want him to. It was as simple—and as complicated—as that.

Shelby shook her head again. No, she didn't want him to leave.

One corner of his mouth tilted in a smile before he claimed her mouth in a crushing kiss. Again his body demanded she respond and she eagerly complied, her hands running across his chest and down, sliding around his waist to draw him closer.

And brushing against the gun secured in the back of his waistband. She jerked her hands back and held them at her sides, the feel of the cold steel still burning her palms. She felt him smile against her neck as his mouth grazed her skin, his breath hot as he spoke.

"Don't worry, the safety's on."

"No." The word came out as a croak and she cleared her throat. "No, it's not that. It's..." Her voice trailed off. How could she explain that it wasn't the gun, but the reminder that they were two completely different people, from two completely different worlds? That it was a reminder that she wasn't who he thought she was?

Josh pulled away, his gaze steady and understanding despite the harsh rise and fall of his chest, despite the rapid beating of the pulse in his neck. "Tell me, Shelby. What is it? Would you be more comfortable if I took it off?"

She shook her head, touched at his willingness to make her feel at ease even if he misunderstood her reason for it. "No, it's not that. It's...I'm not who you think I am."

Josh stepped back and studied her, then raised his brows in question. "And who is that I think you are?"

"Friday night. I'm not that woman."

"You're not?"

Shelby shook her head and looked down at the floor. She heard something that resembled a choking sound come from Josh, and was afraid to look up at him. But his hand tightened around hers and pulled her forward, not stopping until he reached the sofa. He motioned for her to sit, then reached around and pulled the holster from the back of his pants.

He sat the gun on the coffee table, following it with a black pouch that contained handcuffs and then the clip that held his badge. Her eyes focused on the items even as he lowered himself next to her, taking her hands in his.

"The safety is on and it's not going to accidentally discharge, but I understand if the gun bothers you—"

"No, really, it's not the gun."

"Are you sure? Because some people get freaked out about them."

"I'm sure. It's not the gun."

"It's because you're not who I think you are. Is that it?" Shelby nodded, her gaze still on the table. "The woman from Friday night, right?"

Shelby nodded again. Several minutes of silence stretched around them, so unnerving that she finally looked up.

And saw the rakish smile on his face as he studied her.

"So who was I with Friday night? Because I'm pretty sure I was with you."

"But that wasn't me. I mean, it was me, but I'm not...I've never done anything like that before."

"Like what? Pick up a stranger in a bar?"

Shelby's face flamed in embarrassment at the admission, but she nodded. "That and...everything else. That wasn't really me."

Josh's smile grew bigger as he stared at her for a long minute. Then he leaned closer and reached around, tugging the holder from her pony tail and tossing it onto the coffee table. He ran his fingers through her hair, spreading it out across her shoulders before giving her a long kiss.

"Sweetheart, as for picking up strangers in a bar, I knew that night that was something new for you. If I hadn't, I wouldn't have taken you with me."

Shelby's eyes widened at his words. How could he have known? Maybe he was just saying that, to make her feel better. She continued watching him, her breathing coming faster as he inched closer, his gaze intent on her parted lips.

"As for the other stuff...I think it *was* you. At least, how you are with me. How we are together."

"But—"

Josh silenced her with his mouth, his kiss gentle and coaxing at first, slowly drawing her forward, bringing to life the fire that smoldered deep inside her. She met each thrust of his tongue, leaning closer and closer, until her body pressed flush against his.

And then the fire erupted, consuming her, and she wanted more. Needed more. She ran her hands up his arms and across his chest, impatient with the barrier of clothes separating them. She pulled at his shirt, freeing it from his jeans and tugging it up, letting him take it off so she could focus her touch on his chest.

Shelby moved even closer, throwing one leg over his lap until she was straddling him, her mouth trailing kisses along his neck and chest as her hands roamed over his heated flesh. Her finger outlined the scar and she paused, studying it again, awareness of his job giving it new meaning. She glanced up at him, silently questioning.

"Bad guy with a knife." She narrowed her eyes, filled with a sudden urge to find the bad guy and do him bodily harm. Her thoughts must have shown on her face, because Josh smiled at her, passion darkening his eyes even more. "Bad guy got his."

"Good." Shelby nodded then lowered her head, tracing the ragged line with her tongue. Josh's breath hitched in his chest and a small groan fell from his lips, emboldening her. She moved lower, her mouth and hands and tongue covering every inch of his chest and flat abs, not stopping even when she reached his jeans.

Her hand glided down his thigh, squeezing the hard flesh under the soft denim, sliding back up to run across the hard bulge straining against his zipper. Shelby looked up at his soft groan. His head was thrown back, his jaw clenched as he slowly pressed his hips against her palm.

She unsnapped his jeans and tugged at the zipper, easing it down slowly, teasing him with her hand one inch at a time until she reached in and pulled him free. She lowered herself to the floor in front of him, watching his face as she stroked him, long hard strokes from the tip of his cock all the way down to the base.

Shelby leaned forward, following the stroke of her hand with her tongue, kissing his full sack before pulling it into her mouth as she ran her hand up and down the hard length of his cock. His hips thrust forward as he groaned again on a long sigh, and suddenly it wasn't enough. She wanted more from him. She wanted to make this man pant with need, to make him feel just a fraction of what she felt.

Shelby gave his sack one last teasing lick, then ran her tongue up his shaft, twirling it around the smooth tip before closing her mouth over him. Slowly, inch by inch, she took him in, teasing with her tongue and hand as she sucked him.

His hands closed in her hair, his fingers twisting in the strands as his hips thrust against her mouth. She increased her rhythm, feeling the dampness spread between her own legs as she pleased him.

"Shelby..." He uttered her name in a hoarse growl, his hands tightening in her hair as she sucked, harder, deeper, taking all of him in. "Oh God, Shelby..."

She looked up and met his dark gaze, his eyes

glazed with passion as he watched her suck him. A heady sense of power filled her and desire coiled even tighter in her, sending more wetness between her legs to dampen her sweat shorts. Her muscles tightened and quivered, encouraging her as much as the look in his eyes.

She ran her tongue up one side and down the other, stroking him again then taking him back into her mouth. The thrusting of his hips became more urgent even as he tugged at her hair, trying to pull her away as he shook his head. "Shelby, no—"

She freed his hands from her hair and took more of him in, feeling the tip of his cock touch the back of her throat. His sack contracted under her touch and a low groan escaped his mouth. She wrapped one arm around his hips and held him closer, refusing to let him pull away as she went faster, harder, deeper.

His hands gripped her head again, this time holding her in place instead of pushing her away. His hips thrust once, twice, her name ripped from his lips in a hoarse groan as he finally let go.

**

Josh's chest heaved with heavy breaths and a shudder went through him as Shelby finally released him. He closed his eyes and threw his head back against the sofa, searching for control.

Control. Christ, he never gave up control like that. Never. He growled and reached for her, dragging her up off the floor and pulling her across his lap before crushing his mouth to hers. To his surprise, she turned her head away and looked up at him, a surprising shyness in her eyes.

"No. I mean, not after—"

"Bullshit." The word came out as a growl that he thought might have scared her if not for the look of pleasant surprise in her eyes. He lowered his mouth to hers and swept his tongue inside, tasting his own saltiness mingled with a pure sweetness in the recesses of her mouth.

He pulled at her shirt, yanking it off her with no thought of gentle seduction. He shifted slightly, moving so she was stretched across the sofa, and ran his hand slowly down her body until he grabbed the waistband of her deliciously short sweatpants and dragged them down her legs. And yes, thank you Jesus, that was all she was wearing.

He ran his hand back up her thigh, watching her face as he cupped her in his palm, running his finger across her short curls and down her clit before sliding inside her. "You are so wet. So silky wet."

Her eyes fluttered open and her gaze met his, shyness mingled with bold desire as she watched him. He reached out and twined his fingers with hers, then dragged their clasped hands down across her body. "Touch yourself for me. See how wet you are."

He guided her finger to her clit, then leaned back and watched as she stroked herself. Her eyes closed and her head fell back, her finger sliding up and down, pleasuring herself as he continued to stroke her from the inside.

She spread her legs even further and reached down with her other hand, opening herself even further to him. His cock hardened instantly in response, the throbbing nearly painful as he watched her, learning where she liked to be touched the most. Her head turned to the side, her mouth parting as her chest rose and fell with rapid breaths. Josh plunged two fingers deep inside her, feeling her inner muscles tighten around them, feeling her wetness coat his hand as her hips rocked against his palm.

He dug into his back pocket with his free hand, never taking his eyes off her as he pulled out a wrapped condom. He tore open the package with his teeth and quickly sheathed himself, then shifted so he was braced more fully between her legs. "You are so beautiful, Shelby. Cum for me. Let me see you cum."

He twisted his hand deeper, curling his fingers inside her, and was instantly rewarded with her explosion. Her back arched as a small whimper escaped her parted lips, her head turning from side to side as her hands reached out, searching for him as her hips bucked against his hand.

He shifted, grabbing her hips and sliding her toward him as he raised her legs against his shoulders. He shifted once more and plunged inside her, burying himself to the hilt. Her back arched again, her muscles clenching around his swollen cock, teasing, massaging, coaxing. He eased out of her, slowly, then plunged forward again. Again, faster.

Shelby blindly grabbed for him, her hands closing over his wrists and holding tight. Her head fell back even more as he plunged into her, over and over, faster, each scream and moan from her urging him on.

And still she came for him, her inner muscles contracting, tighter and stronger with each spasm as he rocked into her. He pulled out, held himself away for several long seconds, then drove into her. She arched against him, his name ripped from her lips, over and over as he pounded into her, branding her, marking her as his until his own release exploded in a haze around him.

He tilted his head back and clenched his jaw, his hands still gripping her hips, holding her tight against him as her sweet muscles milked him. The last shudder finally eased from his body. Josh took a deep breath and let it out slowly, then lowered his head, leaning forward and wrapping her legs completely around his waist. He eased his arms around her and pulled her up until he could rest his forehead against her chest. They stayed that way for long minutes, until their harsh breathing quieted around them.

Shelby shifted against him and ran her hand up and down his arm, the touch of her fingers light as a feather against his heated skin. Josh lifted his head and gazed down at her, waiting for her to open her eyes and look up at him. He brushed his lips against hers then shifted, tightening his hold on her as he stood up, pulling her with him. Her legs tightened around his waist and her arms wrapped around his neck, holding on.

He turned and headed toward the back of her apartment, searching for her bedroom as he kept his gaze fixed on hers. "No running away tonight, Shelby. Okay?"

She nodded, a small smile on her face, then settled her head against his neck as he carried her into the bedroom.

And lost a little piece of himself in the process.

Chapter Nine

"Tomorrow night. Six o'clock."

The voice echoed through her haze of concentration, pulling at her. Shelby shook her head and waved the voice away, leaning closer to the tray holding the assorted ammunition. She tilted her head, studying the lead ball, then gently pushed it with the fingertip of her gloved hand.

"What are those things? Bullets?" A bare hand entered her line of vision, nearly touching the misshapen ball; she reached for the hand and grabbed it.

"Don't touch that!" Shelby straightened, keeping a firm grip on the offending limb until she made sure there was no chance of contact. Josh curled his fingers around hers and squeezed, offering her a rakish smile.

"You're so cute with your bug eyes on. Has anyone ever told you that?"

Shelby stepped away from him and quickly pulled off her glasses, her face heating despite the teasing light in his eyes. She placed them on her work table and carefully covered the tray of specimens, then carried them over to the locker and secured it, tucking the key into the pocket of her lab coat.

"So, tomorrow night. Six o'clock. Sound good?"

Her brow creased and she shook her head in confusion. "I don't...what's tomorrow night?"

Josh closed the distance between them and pulled her into his arms, dropping a quick kiss on her lips before smiling down at her. "It's our two-week anniversary. Don't tell me you're already forgetting the important dates. And after everything we've been through together."

Shelby stared at him in blank silence, then realized he was teasing. She laughed but said nothing, not sure how else to respond. A steam roller possessed more subtlety than Josh, and would have surprised her less. He kept her on her toes, never knowing what he would say, what he would do next.

And there had been plenty of surprises so far, she thought, her cheeks flaming with memories. He winked down at her, as if he knew what was going through her mind, then gave her another quick kiss and stepped away. Shelby was thankful for the space, because it gave her a few minutes to compose herself.

Which was the biggest surprise of all, that she had to actually work on composing herself around him. He kept her world tilted. She, who was usually so calm and composed and professional. But not around him. A completely different person emerged whenever Josh was with her, and she had no idea what to make of that.

And it had only been two weeks.

Shelby still wasn't sure what to think of everything. She turned her head to sneak a glance at him as he studied some of the cases in the room, and suddenly realized that he wasn't even supposed to be in here.

And then she realized it must be official business, because he was actually wearing a suit. Well, not a complete suit—navy blue trousers, a white shirt with the top two buttons undone, and a matching blazer with the sleeves pushed halfway up his muscular forearms. He was reaching out to grab an index card from one of the cases. The motion caused his jacket to fall open, revealing his shoulder holster and gun.

Shelby swallowed and looked away, trying to ignore the flush of heat that spread through her at the sight of the firearm. She had read somewhere that some women were attracted to the power of authority, and that still others were turned on by the lethal allure of firearms.

She apparently fell into both categories, because the sight of Josh carrying his gun acted as a powerful aphrodisiac to her.

Putting all thoughts of aphrodisiacs and guns and Josh—especially thoughts of all three together—out of her mind, she made her way around the work table and began tidying up. She stopped halfway through and looked back at Josh, leaning against the wall watching her.

And remembered again that he wasn't supposed to be in here.

"How did you get in here, anyway? This area is supposed to be secure."

He smiled and pulled open the edge of his coat, revealing his badge. "Official business. Besides, I think I scared your security guy. You guys really need to rethink your definition of 'secure' around here."

"Oh." She looked down at the tray in her hands,

then walked to a different storage locker and placed it inside. "You said 'official business'. Have you heard anything about the artifacts?"

His smile disappeared as he straightened, suddenly the professional police sergeant. She easily understood why their poor security guard would have been scared of him. *This* Josh was silently intimidating, exuding a raw power and deadly stillness that caused people to notice...and back away in caution.

So unlike the Josh she had met the first time she saw him.

Well, not the *very* first time...but the first time she met him and realized he was a police officer.

"The Alphabet Soup Group might have a lead. I just had a meeting with Special Agent Levins, and it looks promising. Maybe. They think. Who the hell knows? I'm working on a little investigating myself, just to see if I can light a fire under them. There should be more information by now."

"Oh." Shelby wasn't sure what to think, of any of that. She was still upset and irritated at being made to feel like a suspect. She, who had never so much as gotten a parking ticket. And David still looked at her with a cold calculation in his eyes whenever she had to meet with him, leaving her feeling...tainted and under suspicion. And again she wondered what she had ever seen in him, what mental defect had possessed her and destroyed all common sense.

But that was in the past, something she shouldn't dwell on.

Especially not with Josh standing so close, watching her with that intense gaze of his. That heated gaze...

She shook her head and locked the door to the

cabinet, then grabbed the file log and began jotting down some notes. Josh stepped closer, looking over her shoulder.

"What's that?"

"My file log. I make notes every time a piece is removed: the item number, a description, the time it was removed, why and what was done to it. Just normal documentation stuff."

"Do you do it every time?"

"Every single time, why?"

He leaned further over her shoulder, his brow furrowed in concentration as he read the scribblings. He ran his finger down the sheet, stopping at a line near the bottom. "So you're not the only one who has access then. Does everyone log the information?"

"They're supposed to but...sometimes it doesn't happen."

"Hmph."

"Why? Is something wrong?"

"What? Oh, no." His face cleared and he stepped back, shaking his head. "Just curious."

Shelby thought he was more than just curious but didn't have a chance to question him further because the door opened in a rush. She turned around to see who was in such a hurry to invade her space, then groaned inwardly when David walked in. He stopped mid-stride and stared at Josh, obviously surprised to find him here.

"Sgt. Nichols. My apologies. I didn't realize you were still here. Was there something you needed help with?"

Shelby mentally rolled her eyes and turned away, double-checking the locks before returning the log book to the shelf. She bit back her smile at the change in Josh, who was now standing straight in full intimidation mode as he stared David down.

"No, thank you. I just had a few questions for Dr. Martin."

"I see." David hovered in the doorway, his gray eyes narrowed in suspicion, his cool gaze bouncing back and forth between them. He ran a hand down his thin chest, straightening his tie. He took a step forward, his chest puffed out in self-importance. "I see. Perhaps I should I stay, in case there's something I can help you with."

"That won't be necessary." Josh's tone, in addition to his stance, clearly told David that he should leave. Knowing him as she did, it didn't surprise Shelby at all when David stepped further into the room, insinuating his presence.

She watched the two men from the corner of her eye as she finished cleaning up. David, full of self-importance that masked a lack of confidence, his sense of authority derived from making those around him feel small and unimportant. It was something he did in all of his relationships, both professionally and personally.

Unfortunately, she had experience with both.

Her eyes slid sideways to Josh, so unlike David. His whole being screamed confidence and authority, and he did it by simply...being. She couldn't describe it any other way. He was one of those people who others looked to for answers. She hadn't seen him at work, not really, but she would bet that he was a natural-born leader, someone that others looked up to. His raw power and confidence drew people.

Something she had experienced first-hand. It was what had drawn her to him that night in the bar, a mere two weeks ago.

Her face heated with the memory and she looked away, no longer interested in the power play that was unfolding around her—not when it was a foregone conclusion who would win, not when she had more pleasant things to interest her.

Shelby leaned under the work table and grabbed her tote bag, tossing it over her shoulder as she straightened. The two men could continue facing off if they wanted, but she was eager to leave.

David took a step toward her, blocking her with a stern look. "I'm sorry, but I'm afraid I'll have to check your bag before you leave."

"Excuse me?"

"I need to check your bag. To make sure it doesn't contain museum property, you understand." He gave her a condescending smirk and reached for her tote bag, pulling it off her shoulder before she had a chance to process his words. He had already placed it on the work table and was going through it, removing her personal items, touching them with his pale, sweaty hands before she had a chance to react.

"What are you doing? That's my personal property! You can't do that!" She stepped toward the table and started gathering her things, trying to pile them back into the bag while David tried to pull it away from her.

"I'm sorry, Shelby, but after the recent theft...we just can't be too careful. You were, after all, the last person with them." David tugged, pulling the bag out of her reach, making a show of examining its contents as she stood there in shock. Her mouth snapped closed and her face burned in mortification and shame at the violation.

Josh moved closer, his height dwarfing David. "Excuse me, but are you accusing Dr. Martin of theft?"

David stepped back as if slapped, his mouth opening then closing silently. "Of course not."

"Because I understand that not only was Dr. Martin cleared of any suspicion, she was never really a suspect to begin with. Unless, of course, you have information you're withholding from the authorities investigating this theft?"

"What? No. No, that's ludicrous. Of course not." David shook his head, so flustered at being confronted that he released her bag. Josh shifted. It was a small movement, barely noticeable, but David swallowed and stepped back, obviously anxious to put space between them.

Shelby reached for her bag and started shoveling her things back into it, her hands shaking with a combination of fury and disbelief.

"Well, that's a relief. Slander can be such a costly thing these days, from what I understand. And let's not even talk about the dangers of illegal search and seizure. What a headache." Josh stepped back, a flat grin on his face as he fixed David with a cool look. "Yeah, that's one mess you just want to stay away from. Trust me."

"Illegal.... Of course not. I would never even think to..." David's voice wavered then faded. He took a deep breath, his gaze moving between both of them. He straightened and curtly nodded to Shelby, as if nothing had happened. "Don't forget to lock up when you leave."

Shelby held her breath until he left, the door closing behind him with a loud click. Her shoulders sagged and she turned back to the table, gathering the last of her things. Her hands were shaking so badly that she dropped her notebook. She moved to pick it up, only to be stopped by a gentle hand on her arm.

Josh leaned around her and grabbed the notebook, then placed it carefully inside her bag. He snapped it closed and lifted it from the table, then gently drew the strap over her arm and rested it on her shoulder. His hand stayed there, squeezing in reassurance. The heat from his touch spread through her, comforting, calming.

"You okay?"

Shelby nodded, not quite trusting her voice, then finally looked up at him. Concern burned clear in the depths of his eyes as he watched her, and she offered him a small smile.

"I'm fine, really. He just...I've never had that happen before. It felt...I don't know."

"Like you were violated." It was a statement, not a question. He squeezed her shoulder once more then ran his hand down her arm, taking her hand in his for a brief second before letting go and stepping away. She immediately missed the physical contact, which surprised her because she had never really been completely comfortable with open physical contact in the past. She was the type who had always rolled her eyes and felt embarrassed when she was witness to public displays of affection.

Josh studied her for a long minute, his gaze intense and searching. Shelby wondered what he thought when he looked at her, what he saw. Probably too much. He had a way of taking in everything with a single look, of seeing not only what was there, but what wasn't.

Which made sense, considering his job. But right now, she found it a little unnerving. Like he was seeing into corners of her soul she didn't even know existed.

Whatever thoughts went through his head went unspoken, though. He stepped back and suddenly smiled at her, the laid-back Josh once more. He motioned toward the door, then followed her out of the room and waited while she locked it before taking over and leading her along the hallway.

"So tell me. Has David Spear always been such a pompous asshole?" The question came out of nowhere, completely unexpected, completely irreverent. And completely to the point. Shelby choked back her laugh and glanced around to see if anyone was near who could hear.

But they were the only people in the hallway—not surprising given the hour and the small size of the staff. She let her shoulders relax and gave him a small smile before nodding. "David has always been very impressed with himself, yes. He hasn't quite figured out that not everyone agrees with him."

"Oh trust me, he knows."

"He does?"

"Absolutely."

"So, you're a psychologist, too, hm?"

"No. But part of my job is studying people, watching them, figuring them out. As far as puzzles go, he's pretty easy to solve." Josh pushed open the door and held it for her, then took her elbow as they walked down the steps. "I pity the poor woman who ever finds herself dating him. Talk about esteem issues."

The casual comment caught her off-guard and she stumbled, just a small jerk in her step. She thought she caught herself before he noticed, but Josh stopped and turned to face her. Shelby looked up, trying to turn her face into a carefully blank mask.

"No. Please tell me no." Josh watched her for a few long seconds as her face heated and she looked away, trying to pretend she didn't know what he was talking about. It didn't work, of course. He turned her toward him, stepping just a bit closer. "You actually dated that loser? Temporary insanity, right? You were hit by a car and suffered from brain damage."

"Um, no. To the brain damage part. Maybe." Shelby lowered her gaze, embarrassed to admit that she had, in fact, dated the loser. But there was no excuse she could offer, not even temporary insanity. A few weeks could be called temporary. Some people might be generous and even call a few months temporary.

But a year-long relationship that had ended in a broken engagement? Even she couldn't stretch an insanity plea that far, and she had been the one in the relationship.

Never mind that she realized now that it wasn't really a relationship. At least, not as far as David was concerned. It was convenient for him, a means to an end. *She* was convenient for him, made him look good. Right up until he had undermined her professional reputation in order to secure his promotion—and become her supervisor.

Too bad it had taken her so long to see what her friends had seen from the very beginning.

And what Josh had seen in a matter of minutes.

He watched her now, his dark eyes studying her carefully. Then he smiled and pushed a strand of hair behind her ear, and she forgot all about that lost year.

"Well, I guess we all make mistakes in judgment, right?" He cupped her elbow in his hand as they descended the last few steps. "Are you hungry? Did you want to go grab a bite to eat?"

Shelby paused. Not because of the sudden and unexpected invitation to dinner. No, that wasn't what surprised her.

What surprised her—what worried her—was Josh's comment about mistakes in judgment.

What if she was judging *him* all wrong? Was she making just one more mistake in a series of relationship mistakes?

She mentally shook her head. Relationship? What was she thinking? They didn't have a relationship. At least, she didn't think they did. She had picked him up in a bar, for crying out loud. For a one-night stand. It had been pure coincidence that they had even met again.

But they had. And she had either seen or talked to Josh almost every day since.

That didn't mean they had a relationship.

Shelby didn't know what it meant.

She almost said no. Almost. Maybe they were spending too much time together, for not really knowing what was going on. But did she really need to know? After all, she had picked him up in a bar for the single purpose of, just for once, doing something crazy and fun, just for herself.

That didn't mean it had to stop after one night, right? Maybe she should just look at this like a really long one-night stand.

Something crazy-fun just for herself. She wouldn't read anything into it, wouldn't expect anything from it.

Shelby looked up at Josh, at the smile in his eyes and that rakish grin that did funny things to her insides, and smiled.

"I'd love to."

Chapter Ten

Shelby faced out the window, her eyes scanning the streets as he drove them around. Josh didn't have to see her eyes to know she was looking at everything—her head would turn every now and then to look to her left, or behind them. Curiosity lit her face as she took everything in, letting him know that this was another new experience for.

He sure as hell hoped so, considering they weren't passing through the greatest neighborhoods right now.

He stopped the car at the light, his gaze sliding toward a group of teens hanging on the corner. They noticed his car, noticed him, and moved down the street in the opposite direction. He made a mental note to circle around later, just to check, then turned back to watch Shelby.

She had a beautiful profile, as if her features had been painstakingly, carefully molded from smooth porcelain. Her neck was long and graceful, a temptation to nuzzle and kiss and caress. Not that he could see it right now—the long red curls of her hair covered it from his view. But just because he couldn't see it didn't mean he couldn't appreciate it.

Much like he could appreciate the soft curves of her body, even though she hid them under loose clothes. Not just soft; soft, feminine, fragile, luscious. Some ancient gene in his body roared to life, bringing out an overwhelming need to protect and defend, to fight to the death anyone who would harm her.

Josh didn't think she'd find that as amusing as he did. Then again, maybe she would.

"So. Do you want me to beat him up for you?"

Shelby turned her attention on him, her delicate brows turned down as she obviously tried to figure out who he meant. Her face cleared and she shook her head, turning away.

But not before he saw the faintest blush tinge her cheeks.

"Oh. David. No, that's okay. He's really not worth the trouble."

"No trouble at all, trust me." The light turned, and Josh moved the car forward, driving several blocks in silence. "So...how long ago did you guys break-up? I mean, if you don't mind me asking. I know that's kind of personal and not my business—"

"It's been a while. Over a year ago."

"Oh." Well, that was good. He thought. It meant she wasn't on any kind of emotional rebound. At least, he hoped she wasn't. Although he couldn't imagine why anyone would rebound over that asshole.

His hand clenched around the steering wheel when he remembered how the obnoxious loser had treated Shelby. Deliberately humiliating her, like she was some kind of common criminal. And Josh couldn't shake the feeling that the asshole had actually enjoyed it, like he was putting on a show, flexing some imaginary muscle to put everyone in their place—which was solidly beneath him.

Josh figured he was the worst kind of bully, one who used words and actions instead of fists or weapons in order to make themselves feel more important. And Josh had little patience for bullies...which was just one of the reasons why he was so good at his job.

Another reason he was so good was his ability to read people, and the change in Shelby broadcast loud and clear that she did NOT—in all capital letters—want to discuss her relationship with the guy. And since Josh didn't particularly want her thinking of any guy but him right now, he was happy to oblige.

"Do you have to work this weekend at all?"

Shelby whirled her head toward him, and he knew the change in topic surprised her. No doubt she had expected him to ask more questions about her relationship. Her lips tilted in a small smile and she shook her head.

"No, weekends are generally my own. Once we get closer to opening the new exhibit, I'll be working seven days a week, just to make sure everything goes smoothly. Then, after that—I hope—will come the promotion and..." Shelby trailed off then shrugged before giving him a distracted smile. "Um, no, I don't have to work."

"Promotion, hm? Tell me about it."

"What?" Shelby faced him, her surprise at his interest obvious. She chewed on her lower lip, then finally shrugged, as if making up her mind. "It's nothing big, not really. I'd be doing pretty much the same work, which I love, but I'd also oversee some additional projects. And David wouldn't be my supervisor any longer. Actually, he'd probably have to answer to *me* on some things. Of course, this all depends on the success of the exhibit, so I'm keeping my fingers crossed."

"Sounds exciting. And I'm sure you have nothing to worry about." He reached over and squeezed her hand, then laced his fingers through hers. "Now, back to this weekend. I happen to have this weekend free, too, which is a real treat because it doesn't happen that often. How about we go out on the boat tomorrow night when you get off work? We could go to Annapolis, or just cruise around and maybe anchor out somewhere, just the two of us. What do you think?"

Shelby tilted her head to the side, her dark red brows slashes above her hazel eyes as she studied him, like she was trying to solve a particularly difficult puzzle. And Josh realized he must have come on too strong, that maybe he was pushing too hard, too fast. After all, they hadn't really known each other that long.

It just felt like they did. At least, to him it did. He realized he didn't know what she thought. He had just kind of assumed she felt the same way. Which was stupid, because he knew better than to assume anything.

He almost took the invitation back, or at least thought about rephrasing it a little bit differently, making it sound not quite so presumptuous. But then she gave him a smile, a broad smile that lit her face and eyes and showed a peak of dimple in her cheek.

"Sure, why not? It sounds great. I'd love to."

Josh smiled back, suddenly feeling like a kid allowed to open his birthday presents a day early. But before he could say anything, before he could talk about making plans, activity at the end of the block caught his attention, and he swore under his breath.

He slowed the car and pulled over to the side of the curb, studying the small crowd pouring from the corner bar. He slammed the car into park, still cursing—not just the crowd, but his own sheer stupidity for driving through this particular neighborhood with Shelby in the car.

Josh reached for the radio, making a quick call even as he noticed a patrol car slowing to a stop in the intersection. He exchanged nods with the other officers, then opened the door and got out, quickly removing his jacket and tossing it into the back seat. He leaned in and fixed Shelby with a serious look.

"Stay in the car. Keep the doors locked. And if anything happens, slide behind the wheel and drive."

Her mouth dropped open, a look of surprise and worry creasing her face. But he didn't let her say anything, just slammed the door closed and checked to make sure it was locked before he headed toward the crowd.

**

Shelby watched Josh walk away, his powerful stride carrying him quickly toward the corner. From what she could see, it was just a crowd of maybe twenty or so people gathered outside a building. But Josh had obviously seen something different, or he wouldn't have stopped here and gotten out.

Stay in the car. Keep the doors locked. And if anything happens, slide behind the wheel and drive.

Had he really just told her to drive away if anything happened?

Shelby's pulse raced as she replayed his words in her head. A thin layer of sweat coated her palms. Could this really be dangerous? She leaned closer to the windshield, trying to get a better look. Josh and two other officers were at the edge of the crowd, talking. There was something about the way they stood; in fact, Shelby thought they looked like they were ready to pounce, to move into action at the slightest notice. Even though she hadn't gotten a good look at the other two officers, if she had been confronted by the trio, she would no doubt feel intimidated by them.

Apparently this crowd felt differently, because two of the men stepped forward, confronting the officers. She kept her eyes on Josh, her anxiety increasing as he moved forward.

It happened so fast, she wasn't even sure what happened. One second, there had been a wary stillness among the crowd; the next, pushing and scuffling broke out. Shelby's breath caught in her chest and she reached for the door handle as one man shoved Josh, then bent over and charged him. She saw Josh step back and to the side, saw his arms move outward...

And then, before she could even finish pulling the handle toward her to open the door, it was over. Two men were on the ground, flat on their stomachs, shouting. The crowd thinned out, drifting into the bar or running down the street as two patrol cars turned the corner with squealing tires and wailing sirens.

And Josh was straddling the man who had charged him, pulling his arms back and handcuffing him. He stood up in one smooth and powerful motion, pulling the bad guy up with him.

Shelby released her hold on the door handle and sat back in the seat, her breath quickening. Josh looked over his shoulder at her, and she imagined she could see the dangerous intensity in his eyes. Her pulse raced even faster, her breath coming in short gasps.

Her reaction had nothing to do with anxiety or fear.

No. This was excitement. Pure, hot, intense. It coursed, throbbing, through her body—her veins, her limbs. Between her legs. She shifted, painfully aware of the sudden dampness between her legs, aware of the tightening ache inside her.

Adrenaline rush. She had heard of such things, of the strong sexual arousal that could result from adrenaline-inducing incidents. Nothing more than a physiological reaction.

But oh...my...God. She had never experienced it, had never really understood it.

Until now.

And she didn't want it to go away.

Time disappeared as she sat there, waiting. Minutes maybe, or longer. The feeling didn't disappear. Instead, it increased, growing, the need turning urgent. She noticed movement ahead and looked up. Josh was walking toward her, coming closer.

Her eyes traveled over his body, studying his broad shoulders and chest, his muscled forearms peeking out from the rolled sleeves of his shirt. She lowered her gaze, taking in his lean waist and trim hips and muscled thighs, the palms of her hands tingling at the remembered feel of coarse hair and steely strength under her touch.

Her eyes traveled back up his body as he came even closer, resting on the badge clipped to his waist, moving higher, back to his chest and across...to the lethal gun sticking out from the shoulder holster still strapped around him.

She shifted again, the wet ache between her legs growing stronger. Josh opened the door and slid behind the wheel, turning toward her with an apologetic grin.

"Sorry about that. I didn't expect—" His voice died mid-sentence as he looked at her, his forehead creased in concern. "Shelby? Are you okay?"

"Yes."

He paused, shifted, moved just a little closer as he leaned forward. "Are you sure? You look...Are you upset? Is that it? I'm sorry, I didn't realize—"

"No." Shelby stared straight ahead, wondering how he could possibly think she was upset when she was using every bit of her willpower to stay still, to not move. When all she wanted to do was jump him. Right here.

Right *now*.

"You're starting to worry me, sweetheart. What is it? Tell me what's wrong." Concern laced his voice and he moved even closer. He reached out with his hand, gently running it down her arm. His touch was like lightening, scorching her feverish skin. But she didn't move except to turn her head far enough to look at him. Something of what she was feeling must have shown in her eyes because he stilled, his own dark eyes heating as her gaze held his.

"Could you take me home? Because I'm extremely turned on right now and if you don't, I'm afraid I might jump you. Right here."

He nodded, just a short motion of his head, then jerked the car into gear and drove away.

Chapter Eleven

Holy shit.

The thought tore through his mind for the hundredth time in as many seconds. His hands gripped the sides of Shelby's face, holding her steady as her mouth crashed against his, hungry, devouring. Her hands traveled inside his open shirt, running across his chest and sides, down to his stomach, reaching lower for the button of his trousers. He was pressed between the hard door of her apartment and the soft curves of her body and he shifted, pressing his erection against her eager hips.

They had to get inside her apartment. No, correction. *He* had to get them inside her apartment because right now, he didn't think Shelby cared.

Holy shit.

He pulled his mouth from hers, their harsh breathing loud to his own ears. Shelby groaned then slid her hand into his waistband, her fingers grazing his cock. He drew in a sharp breath and eased her away, before *he* didn't care where they were.

"Shelby, wait. Inside." Her fingers curled around him, soft and teasing against his hardness. Josh clenched his jaw and drew in another sharp breath, then removed her hand and stepped away. "Keys."

She dug in her purse, searching for them by feel as she dragged her mouth along his neck. He grabbed the keys from her, fumbling and nearly dropping them before he found the right one. He jammed it into the hole—yeah, wasn't *that* prophetic—and twisted the door knob, pushing the door open so fast he was surprised it didn't bounce off the wall and come back to hit him.

And then he didn't care, because they were inside, away from nosy neighbors, and Shelby's hands were already busy unzipping his pants. She slid them past his hips, her nails grazing his skin as she kneeled in front of him. He had one brief second of sanity where he remembered to slam the door shut and lock it before her mouth closed over him, taking him in, all of him, and then he didn't care.

Holy shit.

He grabbed her head, his fingers tangling in her thick hair, holding her in place as she sucked and licked him into oblivion. A groan escaped his mouth, low and long, and his head fell back, banging against the door as her tongue swirled around his swollen tip then licked him, all the way to the base, to his aching sack.

Josh tightened his hold in her hair and swiftly pulled her away, leaning forward as he pulled her to her feet, crushing his mouth to hers. Her hands stroked him, wild, frenzied, making him go crazy. He dragged his mouth along her neck, grazing her skin with his lips, his teeth.

Shelby pushed against him, soft against his hard,

her fevered touch pushing him over the edge of reason. He pulled away, his breathing ragged as she ran her hands across his bare stomach, along his ribs and chest, up to his neck and around to his shoulders.

Josh reached between them, his hands reaching for his shirt and shoulder holster to pull both off. Shelby's hands closed over his, stopping him.

"No. I need you. Now. Please." She guided his hands to her hips. His fingers bunched in the material of her skirt, dragging the fabric up, up further until he touched bare skin, until he could slide his hands under the lacy edge of her thong. His fingers skimmed across her trimmed curls and slid into her moist heat.

Her hips surged against his hand, her muscles clenching around his fingers. Shelby's breath was hot and fast against his neck, her nails digging into his shoulders. "Please, Josh. Now."

Holy shit.

He reached for his back pocket, fumbling for his wallet, grabbing it and opening it one-handed. Shelby took it from him, pulling out the condom before tossing the wallet to the side. She ripped open the foil package then reached down between them, rolling it over his hard length.

The heat of her hand against his flesh nearly did him in. He slid his fingers out of her and reached around, cupping her bottom and hoisting her against him. She wrapped her legs high around his waist as he turned and pinned her to the door, driving into her with one swift push.

Her muscles clenched around him, pulling him in deeper. Her head fell back, her soft, quick moans filling his ears as her fingers dug into his shoulders. He shifted, lifting her higher, thrusting into her, impaling her.

She climaxed with a scream, her muscles gripping, squeezing, caressing him as he thrust into her, again and again. Her legs tightened around him, driving the breath from him as he pounded into her, harder, faster.

He should slow down, he *needed* to slow down, but Christ, he couldn't. Her wet heat sheathed him, sheltering him, calling him. Josh braced her more fully against the door and reached up with his hand, pulling at her shirt, tugging at the collar and ripping the top button off in the process. He lowered his mouth to her exposed collarbone, tasting her sweet flesh, kissing with his lips, nipping with his teeth.

She screamed his name, her nails digging into the skin of his shoulders and neck, bucking against him...

Until he exploded deep inside her, his release so powerful his legs nearly buckled under him. And still she rode him, her breath coming in short gasps, her moans filling his ears, slowly fading with the minutes.

Josh filled his lungs with her scent, his chest aching with each breath. The minutes continued to pass, the only sound that of their harsh breathing. He lowered his head to her chest, knowing he needed to move, knowing that she couldn't be comfortable, pinned the way she was.

He couldn't move, not just yet.

He slowly raised his head and opened his eyes, focusing on the soft features of her face, her swollen lips and the damp tendrils of curls that clung to her flushed cheeks. His eyes drifted down, to the long expanse of her neck and the delicate curve of collarbone, to the red marks marring her smooth skin. A surge of possessiveness crashed over him. Yes, he wanted to mark this woman, to brand her as his.

"Shelby." Her name escaped him in a low hoarse growl. Her eyes fluttered open, glazed and unfocused, their color so deep, more green now than hazel, so green he felt like he was drowning in the ocean. He said her name again, then dropped his mouth to hers in a kiss meant to possess, to claim.

He finally pulled away, both of them breathless, and eased his hold on her. She unwrapped her legs and slid down his body. A sigh escaped her parted lips when he slid out of her, but she didn't pull away. Instead, her arms tightened around him. She pressed a small kiss in the hollow of his throat then rested her head against his chest.

Again that feeling of possessiveness swept over him, and his own arms tightened around her.

"Holy shit," he said out loud, feeling her smile against his skin at the words. He pulled away and looked down at her, suddenly worried. "Are you okay? That was a little...intense. I didn't hurt you, did I?"

She almost looked away. In fact, Josh was expecting her to, saw that she wanted to. But she didn't. Instead she met his gaze with her own shy one and shook her head.

"Yes, intense. And no, you didn't hurt me." Then she did lower her gaze. She reached out with one finger and gently traced the curve of his shoulder, still partially covered by his shirt and...Christ, he was still wearing his holster and sidearm. But she didn't seem bothered by it as she continued to stroke his skin, tracing the scratches she had put there. She finally looked back up at him, the shyness of her gaze mixed with something he couldn't quite decipher.

"Are you okay? I didn't mean to...I mean, I didn't realize I was scratching you."

"Sweetheart, if you ever hear me complain about you scratching me, you have permission to pull out my gun and shoot me." He smiled at her, then gave her a quick kiss before pulling her closer, just holding her in his arms.

Another wave of possessiveness washed over him. No, he would never complain about Shelby marking him. In fact, he'd do his damndest to display the brand and proudly call himself hers.

Chapter Twelve

The cafeteria was small, noisy with the clank of pans and utensils, the murmured conversations blending together to create senseless white noise in the dreary room.

But Shelby paid no attention to the activity around her, no longer cared about the cracked gray linoleum and dingy walls painted a pale industrial green. Even the food on the tray in front of her—limp lettuce disguised as salad and a mushy tuna sandwich—couldn't detract from her excitement. She took a sip of the watered-down iced tea and faced Amanda and Chrissy with a smile.

"And we're going out on his boat tomorrow night!"

Amanda smiled at her excitement, but Chrissy just sat there, brooding over her untouched food. She finally blew out her breath and fixed Shelby with such a cool look that she almost pushed away from the table.

"Well hooray for you. Aren't you the lucky one?"

Shelby's smile faltered and she dropped her hands

in her lap, not sure what to make of her friend's sarcasm. Even Amanda looked surprised at the unexpected response.

"Chrissy, what is wrong with you?"

"Nothing. I just hadn't planned on coming here, wasting my lunch hour on this awful slop to listen to Shelby go all gaga over her new boyfriend. Not when I could have had lunch with Gerry instead."

"Gerry? Your boss?"

Chrissy sat up straighter and lifted her chin. "Yes, my boss. Is there anything wrong with that?"

Amanda sipped her water then slid a sly look at Chrissy. "You mean other than he's married and has been trying to sleep with you for the past six months? No, what could possibly be wrong with that?"

"And so what if he does? It's sex, not a relationship." Chrissy turned and gave Shelby a calculating look. "*Some* people know the difference."

"Wow, Chrissy, you really can be a bitch."

Shelby reached out and patted Amanda on the hand, offering her a small smile. "Don't worry, Amanda. I'm not going to let her ruin my mood. I have too much to smile about."

"Yeah, like that mark on your neck? I didn't think you were the kind to walk around with love bites." Chrissy's voice was chilly, almost accusing, and Shelby couldn't understand what had come over her friend. She reached up and adjusted the scarf, looking around to see if anyone had noticed, if anyone had overheard.

"Shelby, you can barely notice it. If you stopped playing with your scarf and fingering it, I wouldn't have even seen it. And I think Chrissy is just showing her jealousy."

"Jealousy? Really? And why, exactly, would I be

jealous?"

Shelby's gaze moved back and forth between her friends, wondering what was going on, wondering if she had missed something. Her face felt warm, no doubt because of the flush caused by Chrissy's comment about her neck. And she had been wrong earlier, because her mood was quickly declining.

"Because you think you're the one who should have left with Josh, not Shelby."

Amanda hissed the accusation at Chrissy, her voice low and strained, determined and shaking. Shelby sat back, speechless. An uncomfortable silence settled over them, none of them speaking, none of them moving. A minute went by, then another, before Chrissy shifted in her chair and cast her gaze down at the table.

"What?" The question came out as a broken whisper and Shelby cleared her throat, finding her voice. "What? Chrissy, is that true? But it was your idea!"

"Yes, it was." Chrissy straightened in the hard plastic chair and fixed Shelby with a level stare. "But I didn't expect you to actually leave with him!"

Shelby continue meeting her gaze, a sudden wary strength filling her each time Chrissy shifted. Amanda was right, Chrissy *was* jealous.

If this conversation—any part of it—had happened a mere two weeks ago, Shelby would have shied away from the conflict. She would have lowered her gaze and mumbled apologies and probably even asked Chrissy for forgiveness, or rushed to her defense in an irrational way to smooth things over. And there was no doubt that Chrissy expected her to do just that, judging from the look in her eyes. And why wouldn't she expect her to do that? It was, after all, what Shelby always did.

But not now, not anymore.

"Amanda's right, Chrissy. You really can be a bitch."

Chrissy stared at her in open-mouth shock as Amanda laughed and clapped her hands. Minutes stretched tight among them and Shelby silently held her breath, waiting to see what Chrissy would do. But instead of getting up and leaving, as Shelby half-expected, she leaned back in her own chair and let out a surprised sigh.

"Well, I didn't see that one coming. I'm surprised." Chrissy folded her arms in front of her and leaned them on the table, tilting her head to the side and studying Shelby—who tried not to squirm under the sudden scrutiny. "Maybe it's a good thing you did leave with him, if he has this kind of effect on you."

Now it was Shelby's turn to shift in the hard plastic chair, uncomfortable at Chrissy's scrutiny, uncomfortable with her words. "What are you talking about?"

"Just what I said. Look at you: you're smiling! Well, at least you *were*. And you're actually excited about something besides work."

"*And* you knocked Chrissy's attitude down a notch." Amanda added before tossing a crouton in her mouth. A grimace flitted across her face, but Shelby didn't know if it was because of the stale crouton, or from Chrissy's shove.

"I have no idea what you two are talking about. And Josh has nothing to do with any of it." A flush crept up her neck and Shelby wondered who she was lying to: her friends, or herself. They must be exaggerating, she thought. She was the same person she was two weeks ago.

Wasn't she?

Of course she was. So what if she felt a little giddy? That just meant she was finally letting go of some of the worry she seemed to always carry around with her. It had nothing to do with Josh. Nothing.

Chrissy pushed her tray to the center of the table and leaned forward. "So tell us about this weekend."

"Well. I'm not sure there's much to tell. Josh has off this weekend, and he asked if I wanted to go out with him on the boat tonight."

Amanda sighed and leaned forward, resting her chin on her hand. "Why can't I meet anyone like that? A romantic evening on a boat. I am so jealous."

Shelby smiled and shook her head, not sure if her friend was teasing or serious. It was just one night on a boat.

Alone.

With Josh.

Shelby could feel her face heat with memories of her last time on Josh's boat. No, it was definitely going to be more than 'just one night on a boat'.

"Are you guys going anywhere special? Or are you going to be just," Chrissy curved her fingers and made air quotes, "'hanging out'?"

Shelby ignored the blush that wouldn't go away and shrugged. "He said something about going to Annapolis and—"

"Shelby. I see you're still here."

David's condescending voice boomed from behind her, startling her. She turned in the seat and had to tilt her head back in order to look up at him. There was no doubt in her mind that he deliberately stood so close to her just so she would have to do exactly that.

Shelby pushed her chair back so she could stand, and was gratified to see him take a step back. And gratified that she was no longer in a position where she had to look up at him.

For anything.

"Yes, David, I am. It's called lunch."

He studied her with his cool gray eyes, his gaze leaving hers and taking in her friends at the table. "I see. Just please be sure that this doesn't interfere with your work. I'm afraid that any additional mishaps might have a...negative...impact on you."

His cold eyes met hers for one brief instant before he turned and walked away, leaving a chill skittering up her spine. She shook her head, certain she was imagining things, then turned to take her seat.

And saw Chrissy giving David's back the middle finger. Shelby laughed before she could stop herself and reached out to push Chrissy's hand down before anyone could see the salute.

"Chrissy, stop. Someone's going to see you."

"Oh please, like I care. Trust me, everyone else here just wishes they could get away with doing it themselves."

Amanda laughed as she piled their half-eaten food onto one tray and wiped the table clean with a napkin. "I still don't know what you saw in him."

"Neither do I," Shelby admitted. "But you know what? I don't care. That was so long ago, it doesn't even matter anymore.

And it was true, she realized. She didn't care. And she hadn't for quite some time. But she had been so wrapped up in...well, nothing really...that she hadn't even admitted it to herself.

Maybe Chrissy was right after all. Maybe Josh *was* having a positive effect on her.

Chapter Thirteen

Shelby looked down at her feet, so focused on her boots that she nearly stumbled. Josh's hand tightened around hers, steadying her as he led them through the crowd. She offered him a warm smile then glanced back down at her feet again.

She loved her new boots.

She loved everything about them—the leather, the weight, the chunky heel, even the chrome accents. Especially the chrome accents. And she really loved the way they made her feel. Full of attitude. Confident. Like she could do anything.

It was a lot like how Josh made her feel. She slid a sideways glance at him and felt her heart trip a little at the sight of his strong profile. Josh had shown up early tonight to pick her up and surprised her with the boots. She had tried to refuse—right after the shock of seeing them had worn off—but he wouldn't take no for an answer, claiming that if she was going to be riding the motorcycle with him, she needed to have the proper footwear.

She had been hesitant at first. The boots were nothing like anything she had ever owned or worn before. But she was helpless to control the sudden excitement and ran into her bedroom to change, taking off her gauzy skirt then digging into the back of her closet to find an old, worn out pair of jeans. She held her breath, hoping they still fit, and breathed a sigh of relief when they did. Then she had to change shirts, deciding on a plain black scoop neck tank that may have been just a bit tighter than what she usually wore.

The sudden flare of heat in Josh's dark eyes when she came back out was all the assurance she needed. The jeans weren't too tight, and the shirt didn't make her look awful.

She looked like she belonged on the back of a motorcycle. She looked like she belonged with *him*.

That thought caused her to stumble again. And again, Josh's hand tightened around hers and he tugged her closer to his side. A devilish smile lifted one corner of his mouth as he looked at her.

"You'll get used to them, don't worry."

Shelby opened her mouth to tell him it wasn't the boots, then closed it again. That was the last thing she could tell him, because then he'd start asking questions.

Questions she couldn't answer. Questions she wasn't even sure she knew the answers to. All she knew, the only thing she kept telling herself, was that they had known each other for two weeks. Fourteen short days.

And she was fairly certain she was falling head over heels for him.

A slight panicky feel washed over her and she pushed it away, refusing to give into it. Two weeks ago, she had made a decision to do one thing for herself.

One wild, daring thing. And if it happened to last for more than the one night she had originally planned on...well then, good for her.

She would not ruin it by second-guessing herself. She would not ruin it by reading too much into something she wasn't even sure was there.

So she offered Josh her own smile, and squeezed the fingers entwined with hers. "I like them. Thank you again for giving them to me. You shouldn't have—"

He silenced her with a kiss. A slow deep kiss that made her toes curl inside her new kick-ass boots. Right there, in the middle of the street, in the middle of the crowds that were gathered for the Canton Block Party.

And it felt right. Oh so right. And Shelby felt like she belonged, like this was the most natural thing for her to be doing. She leaned in closer, running her free hand up Josh's chest, flattening her palm against the soft cotton of his shirt, just above the steady beat of his heart.

Someone jostled them from the side, separating them. Shelby was too entranced by the searching look in Josh's eyes to notice who it was, until someone called her name. Josh's arms tightened around her when she would have turned to see who it was.

"Don't look now, but it's your boss."

She wanted to ask him how he knew, because his gaze never left her. But then she remembered—this was Josh. He was a police officer. Of course he was aware of everything around him. Everything. Even when it didn't appear he was watching, he saw everything.

And he obviously saw the sudden nervousness in her eyes. He gave her an odd look then released his hold on her, stepping back just the smallest bit, putting distance between them as he turned to face David.

The two men eyed each other with a suspicion that was obvious even to Shelby. And although she was tempted to compare the two of them again, she didn't bother.

David couldn't even begin to compare to Josh. She wondered if he realized that, because he quickly looked away from Josh and turned his focus on her.

And failed at hiding his obvious surprise, which was so clear on his face as he eyed her clothing.

"Shelby. I'm surprised. I thought it was you but I was certain I was wrong. To see you dressed like this...and with Sgt. Nichols. Quite surprising." His gaze dashed between the two of them, his mouth pinched in judgment and sour disapproval.

Of course he disapproved. Block parties and casual clothes—and leather motorcycle boots—were beneath him.

Shelby wondered again what she ever saw in him.

And just like at lunch earlier in the day, Shelby realized she didn't care, that it no longer mattered.

With that realization came a new-found freedom, a sense of being released from too-tight bonds. The sensation was liberating. *She* was liberated. Shelby stood up straighter, feeling stronger and more confident than she had in a long time.

"Of course you find it surprising, David. Anything that fails to fit into your narrow-minded mold is surprising to you."

David's pinched face tightened even more, and Shelby swore she heard a choking sound from Josh. But when she looked over at him, his face was carefully expressionless, betraying nothing. And she smiled.

Because she was suddenly free. Because she felt

like she had just turned some corner she hadn't even known was there and that a new life had just started for her. And because, somehow, even though Josh had his cop-face on, she knew what he was thinking, knew that inside, he was laughing. *With* her, not *at* her.

Shelby leaned toward him and raised herself up on her toes to place a quick kiss on his mouth. His left arm came around her and pulled her closer, fitting her hips to his as he quickly deepened the kiss. Behind her, she heard David's huff of disapproval.

"Might I remind you that you are in public, and your behavior is less than professional?"

Shelby pulled her mouth from Josh's but didn't step away from him; instead, she remained close to his side, turning only her head so she could see David. The flare of anger, and something else, in his eyes surprised her but she ignored it.

"And might I remind you, Dr. Spear, that this is my personal time and I am currently not working for you at the moment."

"I would be very careful, Dr. Martin. Very careful. Your job is already in jeopardy. I would hate to see you throw it away completely." He pulled his shoulders back then turned and walked away. A finger of anxiety raced down her back but she shook it away, aided by the gentle squeeze of Josh's arm around her.

Her eyes narrowed on David's retreating back. "I so don't trust him. He's up to something, I know it."

"Why do you say that?"

Shelby shook her head, not quite knowing how to put her feelings into words. "I don't know, just a hunch. I wouldn't put it past him to be involved in this somehow."

"Shelby, if you know something..."

"No, I don't. Like I said, it's just a hunch. Probably just because I don't like him. I really, *really* don't like him."

Josh leaned in and gave her a quick kiss. "My offer still stands, you know. I really will go beat him up for you. All you have to do is say the word."

Shelby smiled at him then shook her head. "He's not worth it. Now tell me...what are we doing here again?"

Josh grabbed her hand and once again led her through the crowd, careful to keep her close as he wound around the moving masses. They had gone almost two blocks before he slowed their pace and finally answered her. "We're meeting up with some of the guys I work with. I told you before—I'm going to take advantage of working a real person's shift while I can."

"You don't usually go out with your friends?"

"No, I do. When I can. But working nights cuts down on the going out."

Shelby nodded, then finally looked around them when she realized they had reached Josh's group of friends. Two things struck her immediately.

The first was that she wouldn't want to meet any of them at night. They might be police officers, but you wouldn't know it to look at them. At least, she wouldn't. They ranged in age from early twenties to upper forties, and in sizes from brawny to burly. Every single one of them exuded the same presence and quiet authority she had noticed in Josh that very first night.

The second thing she noticed was that she was the only date present, which made her more nervous than her first observation. She hung slightly back from Josh, content to stay behind him and out of sight as he greeted everyone. But Josh had other ideas. He stepped to the side and pulled her forward, one hand resting possessively on the small of her back, and introduced her.

"Guys, I want you to meet Dr. Shelby Martin. Shelby, meet the guys."

As far as introductions went, it was pretty low key. That didn't help her nervousness, though—not when every single eye turned to look at her. To say having that much testosterone focused on her all at once was disconcerting would be an understatement.

Despite the intense scrutiny, she didn't detect any animosity, just mild curiosity. After a few seconds, she realized that just as much—if not more—curiosity was directed at Josh. Shelby wondered if it was because he was the only one with a date...or if it was because he didn't usually bring dates.

Although 'date' may have been the wrong word. That's what she was calling this, but maybe Josh thought of it differently. After all, he had simply introduced her as Dr. Shelby Martin. And when it came to drawing from past experiences...she didn't have much. Not with situations quite like this.

Someone pushed a drink into her hand as conversation resumed around her. She caught snippets here and there, and realized that most of them were talking about work.

She sipped the beer, listening some more. No, they weren't just talking about work. Some of them were actually working. Now.

Which may have explained the absence of some other dates, but not why Josh had brought her here.

She sipped more of her beer and studied Josh from the corner of her eye, her pulse automatically kicking up a notch as she looked at him. And was it any wonder why? His rugged good looks, his solid build, his entire being...he just *was*. From the dark hair that curled over his collar to the chiseled sculpture of his face. His dark eyes that either hid all emotion and thought...or burned bright with everything on his mind. And his smiles, from his rakish half-smile that warned of devilish intent to his full smile that slammed into her chest with the force of a wrecking ball.

Shelby noticed he wasn't smiling now. His face was carefully impassive, but his eyes burned with frustration and impatience. He was in deep conversation with several of the other officers, his focus solely on them.

Or so she thought, until he looked over at her. His eyes met hers and held them, the frustration giving way to an impatience of a different kind. The flare of heat she saw in his gaze ignited her from within, searing her. Shelby took a gulp of beer and looked away, trying to hide her flaming face.

Several more minutes went by, time enough for her to regain her composure. From the additional snippets of conversation she overheard, she realized that Josh was in charge of this group of men and that he would normally be working with them, right now.

Except he wasn't working. Because he was baby-sitting.

She raised her head in surprise at the comment and watched him, but he didn't seem to notice. And she wondered if that was why he had brought her tonight. Was he with her because he was supposed to be baby-sitting her? But why?

Hearty laughter from several of the other men in the group stopped her before she could think of a way to ask Josh what he meant by the comment. One of them stepped forward, a broad smile on his face as he shot an appreciative glance in Shelby's direction.

"Hey boss, if you need a break from the babysitting, let me know. I'll volunteer." Several of the others chimed in with their agreement. Shelby looked at them in surprise, realizing they were talking about *her*, and she didn't know if she should be flattered...or worried.

A tense silence fell over the group. She looked over at Josh and realized he was the reason for the sudden quiet. His eyes flared with warning, and a slow tick appeared along his clenched jaw. Shelby tightened her grip on the beer cup and held her breath, waiting...for something.

Josh stepped toward the man who had spoken and the tension within the small group tightened. But just as quickly it disappeared, aided, no doubt, by the sudden lightening of the dark expression on Josh's face. He smiled and shook his head, much like a parent chastising a young child.

"Johnson. Did you just make a play for my girlfriend?"

The man who spoke looked even more uncomfortable. He gave Shelby a nervous glance then looked back at Josh. "Girlfriend?"

"Yes, Johnson. Girlfriend."

"Um, no Sergeant. That is, I didn't mean to, sir. I thought—"

"You thought wrong. My girlfriend does not need a babysitter. Make sure you catch the entire conversation the next time you eavesdrop, Johnson."

"Yes sir."

Josh stepped back and the conversations resumed

once more, punctuated by laughter and male teasing. He turned toward her and gave her a playful wink that made her smile.

But that wasn't the only reason she was smiling. *Girlfriend.*

Josh had called her his girlfriend. Right here, in front of his co-workers. Not just his co-workers, but men who worked *for* him. Men he commanded.

Shelby couldn't help it. Even though she knew it was silly, her smile grew wider. Josh had called her his girlfriend. He moved closer to her and pulled her into his arms, looking down at her with his rakish grin.

"You're not laughing at me, are you?"

"Absolutely not, no." Shelby shook her head and ruined her statement by laughing. Just a little. She bit down on her lower lip to stop the sound.

"It looks like you are to me. Now stop, before you ruin my bad-ass reputation."

Shelby nodded, then laughed some more, helpless to stop herself. Josh growled at her, a real life growl that sent a tingle of excitement down her spine, then lowered his head and claimed her mouth in a kiss.

Right there, in front of everyone. Which Shelby only noticed for the first two seconds before his tongue swept pass the barrier of her lips to dance wildly with her own. She fisted her free hand in his shirt and leaned closer, some small part of her remembering to hold onto the beer cup, knowing she couldn't drop it.

Her breath was ragged and her mind was dazed when Josh finally pulled away, desire shining in his dark eyes as he looked down at her. Her mind slowly kicked back into gear, and she snuck a glance over at the group of police officers.

"Don't worry. Every single one of them will

pretend they didn't see a thing." He whispered the words against her ear, sending another shiver racing across her sensitive flesh. Her eyes slowly focused and sure enough, not a single person looked in their direction—even though they were all smiling as they pretended not to notice.

Josh stepped back, but didn't release her completely. Instead, he kept one arm draped along her shoulders, keeping her close to his side as two of his men walked over to them. His thumb traced a small circle along the flesh at the base of her neck, and she wondered if he did it because he knew what effect that had on her, or if he even realized what he was doing.

"What's the best way to reach you this weekend if we need you?" The question was asked by one of the older officers, a serious-looking man who reminded Shelby of an army sergeant for some reason. Josh shrugged in response, his thumb still tracing those lazy circles.

"Just call my cell. Since I'm officially off-duty, I'm taking advantage of it and taking the boat out this weekend. I figured we'd just go to Annapolis, maybe cruise the bay."

Shelby refused to smile like a simpleton. The idea of spending the weekend on the boat with Josh, just the two of them, away from everything...the idea was still exciting, nearly as exciting as the slow motion of his fingers along the skin of her neck.

She closed her eyes and sighed, reveling in the sensation tingling along her flesh as well as the idea of the two of them, alone, isolated, all weekend.

The two men talked for a few more minutes, but Shelby paid little attention to the quiet exchange of words. She only caught enough to realize that they were working on some kind of investigation, and that Josh was in charge of it. The conversation ended quickly, and Shelby looked up at the silence, only to see Josh looking down at her with an amused expression on his face.

"What?"

He laughed and shook his head, then placed a quick kiss on her temple. "Nothing. You just looked like you were asleep standing up."

"I did?" Shelby dipped her head in embarrassment. Had she really been standing there with her eyes closed? Probably. "Sorry. The neck rub feels too good to resist."

Josh looked from her to his hand, wrapped gently around her neck, his fingers still working at the muscles in her neck. He looked surprised, like he hadn't realized what he was doing, and slowly lowered his hand. Shelby tried not to whimper in disappointment but didn't think she was very successful, not if Josh's smile was an indication.

"I'll have to remember that." He turned back to the small group, telling everyone to have a safe night before taking her hand and heading back into the crowd. He kept them off to the side, away from the heavier foot traffic.

"So, about this weekend..." His voice trailed off and Shelby looked over at him. He kept his gaze straight ahead, aware of the crowds and the path they were taking, but she could still see the uncertainty in his expression. "I know I had asked about tonight, but I never mentioned the whole weekend. And I was hoping...do you have any plans until Monday morning?"

"Actually, I do."

"Oh. Of course you do. Stupid. That's what I get for—"

"I was planning on spending it on a boat with this really hot guy I just met."

Josh came to a stop, only to be jostled from behind. He looked around them then moved out of the crowd, stopping against the side of a building so they wouldn't be run into. He braced one hand against the brick wall, just above her head, and looked down at her with a small smile.

"A really hot guy, huh?"

Shelby shrugged. "I think so."

"Hm. I don't know about that 'just met' part, though. As a police officer, I have to warn you about the dangers of going off with strangers."

"But he's not a stranger. At least, he doesn't feel like one." Shelby reached out with one hand and trailed the tip of her finger across his collarbone and slowly down his chest. "In fact, I feel pretty safe with him."

"Safe? Sounds boring to me."

Shelby dragged her finger lower, easing her way past his chest, along the tight ridges of his hard stomach, tracing the line of hair that she knew was there but that she couldn't see through his shirt. A smile teased the corners of her mouth when the muscles of Josh's abs twitched under her teasing touch. She ran her finger along the waistband of his jeans, then slowly let her hand drop away before looking back up at him.

"He is most definitely not boring. In fact, I find him extremely exciting."

Josh's gaze burned into hers, hot with sudden desire, his husky voice exciting her even more. "Is that a fact?"

"That is most definitely a fact."

His gaze continued to sear her, intense, open. He shook his head then leaned forward, his mouth closing over hers in a fiercely heated but too short kiss.

"You have no idea what you do to me, woman. C'mon, let's get out of here." He grabbed her hand again and pushed back into the crowd, his pace faster than before. Shelby matched his stride, just as eager to leave, already anticipating riding behind him on the motorcycle.

And anticipating the weekend to come.

Chapter Fourteen

Josh was in trouble. He knew it as surely as he knew his name, rank, and badge number.

What he didn't know was: what was he going to do about it? Better question: did he want to do anything about it at all?

Yeah, that was definitely the better question.

He shifted his position on the berth and pushed up to one elbow, cradling his head in his hand as he stared at Shelby. She was sound asleep next to him, her thick hair curling wildly around her soft face and smooth shoulder. One of her arms disappeared under the pillow; the other curved over her chest, her hand curled loosely under her chin. Josh watched the rise and fall of her chest with each slow breath she took. The long fringes of her lashes were a dark contrast against her pale skin. Her mouth, with those full, kissable lips, parted slightly in sleep.

Blood rushed to his cock, hardening his length as he recalled everything those lips were capable of doing to him. Everything this woman was capable of doing to him.

For shit's sake, he was stretched out beside her, watching the soft rays of the new sun caress her lush body with the gentleness of a lover's touch. Just watching.

That in itself was enough to let him know he was in trouble. Not the watching part. What sane man wouldn't find pleasure in studying her lush body, soft with sleep, bathed in a new day's light?

No, it wasn't the watching part that worried him. What worried him, what really let him know he was in trouble, was the fact that he was content to watch. And apparently wax poetic about it at the same time. Holy hell, he was lying there with a raging hard on and all he wanted to do was...watch her sleep.

Josh closed his eyes and ran his free hand over his face with a sigh, wondering what had gotten into him. He had never let a woman get to him like this. Never. He didn't have time for relationships, not with his schedule, not with his line of work. Hell, he wasn't even in the market for a relationship. Too many of his friends had suffered from broken relationships, shattered as a result of long hours and the stress of the job. So he made sure that whatever relationships he did have were casual. No strings attached, no promises.

And he never introduced any of his dates to anyone from work. Never. The fact that he had introduced Shelby to his guys Friday night, that he called her his girlfriend and publicly laid claim to her right there in the middle of the street, told him something.

He just hadn't figured out what that something was yet. Yeah, he wanted to show her off. But it went beyond that. How far beyond he didn't know.

Far enough, though, that he knew he didn't want this to end. Not anytime soon. The last two days had gone by too quickly. In a few hours, they would pull-up anchor and head back to the marina. Night would fall and Monday would come before he realized it.

And he didn't want it to. Because he knew that, unless something else happened in the next few days in the case of Shelby's missing artifacts, he would be pulled as liaison this week and go back to his regular assignment.

Which would make seeing her difficult at best, considering he usually worked night shifts. That was when his vice squad did their best work.

The fact that nothing had turned up about the artifacts bothered him. Two weeks had gone by, and nothing. He had checked with Special Agent Levins on Friday before picking up Shelby, and he was bothered by the lack of leads as well. There should have been something by now. A whisper on the black market, a clue, some hint of where they were, or at least why they went missing. Josh's instincts screamed that he was missing something, that there was something there that he should be seeing, but it hovered just out of his reach.

And by the end of the week, it wouldn't matter, because it would no longer be his problem. He would no longer be liaison, and things would go back to business as usual. And business as usual would mean not being able to see Shelby, not with his schedule.

And for the first time in a long time—no, the first time ever—he resented his version of business as usual.

Yeah, he was in trouble.

He ran his hand over his face again and let out another sigh, then turned back to watch Shelby. His eye caught on the splash of red, brown and blue tucked behind her pillow and he smiled. Her sock monkey. A silly, childish stuffed sock wearing a blue jersey proclaiming Navy Football. He had no idea what had possessed him to buy it for her. He had seen her looking at it as they walked past one of the many little shops in downtown Annapolis yesterday. Shelby had given it just a quick look, barely more than a passing glance, but her face had lit up with a wide smile when she saw it.

So he had gone back and bought it for her, surprising her with it. The emotion in her eyes when he presented her with it had been worth it.

He smiled at the memory and looked back down at Shelby. Thinking about what the weeks ahead might bring was a waste of time right now. It did no good to think about what might happen, not when she was with him now. He had no intention of wasting today worrying about tomorrow.

He reached out with his hand and drew his finger lightly along her collarbone, feeling the softness of her skin under his touch. Her mouth tilted up, just the smallest bit, then relaxed again in sleep. He continued the path from her collarbone to her shoulder then down her arm, smiling when her mouth tilted up again. His hand finally reached hers, his fingers tracing the delicate bones of her own, before moving back up and gently caressing her lower lip with the lightest of touches.

Shelby's eyes fluttered open, her gaze still filled with sleep as her eyes slowly focused on him. She blinked then offered him a sleepy smile that made him catch his breath, as if he had just been kicked in the gut.

He swallowed, then smiled back at her. "Hey."

"Hey."

"I didn't mean to wake you up." Which was a huge lie. The look on Shelby's face let him know she knew it, too. But she smiled again and grabbed his hand with hers, twining their fingers together.

"You look like you're deep in thought. What's wrong?"

"Nothing. I'm just enjoying watching you sleep."

She studied him for a long second and he wondered if she believed him about the nothing-being-wrong part. But she didn't say anything, didn't question him. Instead, she ran her sleepy gaze across his body, down his chest and lower, coming to a stop at his very obvious hard-on, standing at attention just for her. She brought her gaze back up and when she met his eyes again, the last fog of sleep was gone, replaced by a mix of feminine awareness and shyness that he found irresistible.

Josh leaned forward, his gaze holding her captive until he pressed his lips against hers. He tugged his hands from hers, using his fingers to trace the line of her jaw, moving up to cradle her cheek in his palm as he deepened the kiss. Slow and deep, he took his time, savoring her taste, breathing in her soft sigh as his tongue explored the recesses of her mouth.

Her hand curled around the back of his neck, pulling him closer. He shifted, moving over her, feeling her soft curves mold against the length of his body. Another sigh escaped her, a small moan of contentment as her hips lifted toward his, searching.

It would be so easy to plunge inside her, to drive deep and feel her wet warmth welcome him, sheath him. But Josh was having none of that. Not now, not yet. He wanted to make love to her in the rays of the rising sun spilling through the open hatch. He wanted to cradle her in his arms and feel her come alive under him as the waves made soft music against the hull beneath them.

He gentled the kiss and slowly pulled away, gazing down into her eyes, and felt himself drowning in their depths. He ran his fingers through her hair, pushing the soft strands away from her face, reveling in the feel of silk against his skin.

Her eyes drifted shut on a soft sigh, and he leaned closer to tease her bottom lip with his teeth. "Look at me, Shelby."

She didn't listen right away, and he teased her bottom lip again until her eyes finally opened. The emotion he saw in their depths before she could hide it shattered his resolve, and he knew again that he was in trouble.

He wanted this woman. Not just for sex, and for more than making love. He wanted *her*.

He *needed* her.

With a fierce groan that surprised even him, he caught her mouth in a possessive kiss that left no doubt about how he felt. He was unable to put a name to it—no, he refused to put a name to it—but he was helpless to stop his body from letting her know.

Her own body replied in kind, wordlessly, as her hands roamed across his back and shoulders. They drifted down his arms then back up until she cradled his face between her palms, pulling him even closer.

Josh reached blindly beside him, his hand finally closing on a wrapped condom. He fumbled with the package, then shifted so he could sheath himself, his lips never leaving hers. And still he waited, resisting the urge to drive deeply into her.

But Shelby had other ideas. She pulled her mouth away from his and looked into his eyes, her gaze misty, the color even deeper than before. "I need you inside me, Josh. Please. Make love to me."

And his resolve shattered. He clasped both of her hands in each of his and held them loosely above her head. He stretched his body along the length of hers and poised himself at her moist opening. Keeping his eyes locked on hers, he eased himself inside her, slowly, torturing himself with the wait.

Shelby's eyes drifted shut and he stopped, holding himself painfully still. "Look at me, Shelby." Her eyes finally opened, the flash of emotion once more clear before she blinked it away. He held her gaze and inched his length into her warmth, still moving slowly, so slowly until he was completely buried inside her.

She moved her hips against him, her teeth pulling on her lower lip as she surged upward. He pulled back and shook his head, just the smallest movement, letting her know without words that he was setting the pace.

And he did. Slow, ever so slow, torturing them both until her tight sheath clenched around him, pulling him in deeper. Shelby's head fell back and her hands squeezed his. Her ragged breathing changed to hoarse moans as her orgasm exploded in a waterfall of wet heat. Her inner muscles tightened around him, clenching, demanding.

Josh lowered his head and claimed her mouth with heat and urgency, finally giving in, driving into her until his own climax exploded deep inside her. And still she cradled him, pulling him even deeper inside, draining him until he collapsed on top of her.

Their harsh breathing mingled together and

echoed around them, slowly fading into the sounds of the waves beneath them. The morning call of the seagulls greeting the new day drifted through the hatchway, their normally harsh screech muted inside the intimate confines of the main berth. Josh moved to the side then wrapped his arms around Shelby, pulling her tight against him. He smiled at her sigh of contentment and tightened his hold on her as she snuggled against him, the length of their bodies touching, their legs entwined together.

Yeah, Josh was in trouble. But he couldn't help thinking that this was the kind of trouble he would gladly accept.

Chapter Fifteen

Shelby glided through the doorway. She stopped just inside the entrance, her head tilted to the side, thinking. Yes, she was definitely gliding. If she wasn't careful, she'd soon be skipping and humming as well.

A small laugh escaped her lips and she looked around to see if anyone noticed. The lobby entrance was surprisingly empty, unusual for a Monday morning. For any morning, actually. She shrugged, refusing to let something so minor worry her, not when the day had started out so perfectly.

Yes, she thought, waking up in Josh's arms definitely started the day on a perfect note. If she wasn't careful, it could quickly become a habit she wouldn't want to break.

She refused to let that bother her as well—the worry over whether or not spending so much time with him had already become a habit. The weekend had been perfect, just the two of them out on the boat. And neither one of them wanted it to end. Some unspoken agreement had passed between them when Josh finally docked the boat. He had taken her back to his place on the motorcycle, picked up his suit for a court hearing this morning, and taken her back to her place.

Where he had stayed the night, holding her close after making love to her. Again.

It felt like she had known Josh for a lifetime instead of only a couple of weeks. Any other time, that would have worried her. But not today. Not anymore.

Shelby smiled to herself and continued through the lobby, making her way through the quiet hallways to the far corner of the building where her office was located. Today would be a busy day, cataloguing the remaining pieces that had come in for the exhibit. When that was done, she would put the finishing touches on the final preparations for each display. She was actually ahead of schedule for the opening in a few weeks, and she hoped it stayed that way.

Except for the missing artifacts, everything was going smoothly. And the missing artifacts still bothered her. Why would anyone steal them? She and Josh had talked about it briefly, and even he seemed confused about it. But she hadn't asked him for details, worried that he shouldn't be discussing things with her.

Shelby turned the final corner to her hallway and slowed her footsteps at the sight of the people gathered around her door. David stood facing her, a look of smug triumph on his face when he saw her. One of the museum's security guards stood to his left. To his right was a police officer, a hard-looking man who seemed carved of granite. Shelby closed the distance between them, stopping several feet away. The door to her office stood wide open. She glanced inside before pulling her bag higher on her shoulder and turning to David.

"What is going on here? Why is my office unlocked?"

"I unlocked it. And I found some interesting things inside."

"What are you talking about?"

"Officer, this is Dr. Shelby Martin. I'm sure you'll discover soon enough that she was the one responsible for taking the artifacts."

"What?" Shelby made no attempt to hide her outrage. Seething inside, she glared at David, refusing to give voice to every insult that bounded through her mind. She glanced over at the security guard, a young kid she knew still lived at home, who had always offered her a shy smile whenever she walked by. His gaze was now fixed on the floor, studying his scuffed boots as he shuffled from one foot to the next.

She turned toward the police officer, feeling the first twinge of dread at his hard impassive face. He looked worn and tired, determined and unforgiving. For the first time, a shiver of apprehension pebbled her skin.

Shelby turned back to David, her palm itching to slap the condescending smirk from his face. "How dare you! This is absolutely ridiculous! I did no such thing and you know it. What are you up to, David? What are you trying to do?"

"Officer, you can clearly see the missing artifacts on her desk. Shouldn't you be arresting her?"

"What?" Shelby spun around and looked back into her office, her gaze going directly to her desk. It couldn't be possible. But her own eyes wouldn't lie to her. There, sitting in the middle of her desk, were the missing pieces.

A small wooden frame stood in the center, a piece

of 151-year-old glass the only thing protecting the fragile lock of hair taken from President Abraham Lincoln during the autopsy after his assassination. Next to it, sealed in a specimen round, were fragments of the bullet that had ended the President's life.

She took a step toward her office, not believing her eyes and needing to get closer, to see if they were real or not. The officer stepped in front of her, blocking her way.

"I'm sorry ma'am, but I can't let you in there."

"It's *Doctor*." Her words came out harsher than she intended, and the officer's gaze changed from cool disinterest to hard suspicion in the second it took her to regret speaking. She heard David snicker behind her and she whirled around, ready to attack.

Something flashed in his eyes as she stepped toward him, gone in a quick second. But not before she could see it, not before the pieces clicked into place and she realized exactly what had happened. She took another step toward him, ready to lash out.

"You! Oh my God, it was you!"

"I don't know what you're talking about." David stepped away from her, the condescending smirk still on his face. Shelby advanced on him, her fist curling by her side, her anger bubbling just below the surface.

She didn't think she would actually hit him, as much as she wanted to. But he put his hand out to stop her advancing, pushing against her shoulder. She swatted his arm away, swinging harder than she intended. The officer grabbed her arm from behind and she whirled on him, trying to pull free from the vice grip that was his hand clasped around her upper arm. His hold tightened even more and she winced in pain as she finally pulled free from his punishing grip.

The heel of her shoe caught on the hem of her skirt, tripping her. Shelby wheeled backwards, trying to catch her balance as she started falling, but there was nothing there to stop her, nobody there to help her. She fell to the ground, her cheek making contact against the tile with a loud smack, her bag digging into her ribs with a sharp pain that knocked the breath from her.

And suddenly she was on her stomach, a heavy weight pressed firmly in the middle of her back. Her bag was ripped off her shoulder with a wrenching tug and both arms were pulled roughly behind her, making her cry out in pain.

"You're under arrest..." The remaining words disappeared in a fog of pain and humiliation, hurt and fear, as Shelby bit back tears, wondering what was going to happen next.

Chapter Sixteen

"Where is she? Where in the hell is she?" Josh stormed through the corridor of the precinct, his shout loud enough to bounce off the walls and halt everyone within hearing distance. He was furious. No, he was beyond furious, ready to do bodily damage to anyone foolish enough to get in his way. He turned the corner and stopped, his gaze searching for someone, anyone, who still possessed an ounce of sanity in this suddenly insane building.

Because that was the only excuse he could think of to explain why Shelby had been arrested.

He spotted several of his men standing near the doorway that led to the interrogation rooms. They straightened at his approach and he waited until he was closer before speaking.

"I want to know what the hell is going on and I want to know now." He kept his voice low and even, controlling the fury that burned inside him. Johnson pushed away from the wall and stepped closer, keeping his voice low to avoid being overheard.

"She's in one of the interrogation rooms for now, with charges pending against her. A couple of us happened to be listening to the radio when Officer Dillon called her name in for a check after he arrested her. We barely made it to Central Booking before him to stop him, and had him bring her here instead."

Josh clenched his jaw tight, the seething fury growing. The thought of Shelby even being near the hell that was Central Booking made his stomach clench and heave. The idea of rough hands strip searching her, treating her like a common criminal, reducing her to nothing more than a number on a report before throwing her in with the animals that prowled the streets of Baltimore...he swallowed against the sour bile that bubbled up from his gut.

And he thanked God, not for the first time since listening to his voicemail, that his men had heard. He thanked God that he had taken Shelby out Friday night, that he had introduced her to them, that he had claimed her as his girlfriend in front of them.

He didn't want to think about what she would be enduring right now if he hadn't. He didn't want to think about what she had already endured in the four hours since her arrest.

"Dillon isn't budging on the charges. But there's no way they'll stick. It's become a power play, and he's making noise about our interference."

"Let him make all the noise he wants. He won't be saying much of anything by the time I'm through with him." Josh took a deep breath, trying to force an outward calm before he went through the door. He moved, intending to reach for the doorknob, and was surprised when Johnson stepped in front of him.

"Boss, two things before you go in...the

lieutenant's looking for you. He wanted to see you as soon as you got here."

"Fuck him. I'll see him when I'm done. What's the second thing?"

"Um...she's pretty...I mean, I don't think it's as bad—"

"Sgt. Nichols. A word. Now."

Josh turned from the suddenly uncomfortable Johnson, wondering what he was trying to say, and came face-to-face with his lieutenant. He came close, very close, to disobeying a direct order, his need to see Shelby nearly uncontrollable.

But something in the lieutenant's eyes stopped him. Josh clenched his jaw tight, his back teeth grinding under the pressure, and motioned for his men to stay there before following the lieutenant into an empty office that was being used for storage.

The lieutenant closed the door with a soft click and stared at him for a long minute. Josh made no attempt to hide his impatience or his anger at being stopped. Lt. Adams finally nodded, then folded his arms across his chest and fixed Josh with a steady gaze.

"The theft charges have already been dropped."

"Theft? For what?"

"The artifacts that went missing showed up on her desk this morning. The museum's director claims to have had a hunch and decided to search her office again this morning. He claims to have found them locked in a desk drawer."

"Bullshit. She was never a suspect in their disappearance to begin with. And he's saying...what? That he broke into her office and just found them there? By pure dumb luck."

Lt. Adams held up his hand, calmly stopping

Josh's raising voice. "No. He's claiming she snuck in over the weekend and hid them in her office."

"That's bullshit, sir. I was with her the entire weekend. From the time she left work Friday evening until I dropped her off there this morning. I can alibi her the entire time."

The lieutenant stared at him, his gaze thoughtful but revealing nothing. He leaned against the empty desk, his eyes carefully watching Josh.

"That's interesting, because she claims to have nobody who can vouch for her whereabouts this weekend."

That information hit Josh like a punch in the gut, just one more blow he wasn't prepared for today. Why in the hell would Shelby tell anyone that? Why wouldn't she let everyone know she was with him?

The only reason he could imagine would be to protect him. That she was worried he would get into trouble over it for some reason. As soon as the realization came to him, he knew that was exactly something Shelby would do. And he didn't know if he should kiss her for her loyalty...or shake some sense into her. But first, he had to get her released.

"Sir. Shelby was with me the entire weekend, out on the boat. We stopped in Annapolis for crabs. I'm sure I can find—"

"I believe you, Josh. That's not an issue, anyway, because the theft is not an issue."

"Then I need to get her out of—"

"The other charges are a little more difficult. Officer Dillon is refusing to budge on them."

"What other charges?" Josh realized that Johnson had said much the same thing, but he had thought they were all related to the ridiculous theft charges.

"Assaulting a police officer and resisting arrest."

"What?" The question came out in an outraged bellow. Shelby? *His* Shelby? Assaulting and resisting? There was no way. The lieutenant held up his hand again, stopping Josh before he could even get started.

"I'm inclined to think the charges have a very...shall we say...weak basis to them. But again, Officer Dillon is being adamant. I called to have the security tapes pulled right after I heard, which was only a half-hour ago. I wanted you to know that before you go in there. I also wanted you to know that, if your men weren't quite so loyal, I could have acted much sooner on this whole issue."

"Yes sir. Thank you." Josh nodded, not knowing what else to say, only knowing that his men, from his lieutenant down, had his back. He turned around, anxious to leave, anxious to get in and see Shelby.

"One more thing, Sergeant." Josh paused and looked over his shoulder, noticing the warning light in Tom's eyes. "Do not do anything in there that I cannot fix later."

Josh acknowledged him with a short nod then walked out of the room, his angry stride tearing up the short distance to the interrogation rooms. His men still waited for him and he nodded briefly at them, letting them know everything was okay before pushing past them. He saw Johnson open his mouth to say something but he shook his head and kept going, pulling open the door with an angry jerk, worrying only about reaching Shelby.

The interrogation rooms were nothing more than interconnected offices, two on each side. Josh went immediately to the closed door on the left. He took a deep breath, trying to calm himself, striving for a carefully blank expression before he entered.

What he wanted to do was throw open the door with a loud crash and tear into Officer Dillon with both fists. But that would no doubt scare Shelby even more, and alert Dillon to his intentions. Better to enter calmly and quietly.

He took one last long deep breath and slowly opened the door. His gaze swept the room, resting for a long minute on the smug face of Officer Dillon before moving to Shelby.

One quick glance at her was enough to snap his resolve. He took two steps into the room then reached behind him and slammed the door shut. He saw Shelby flinch, but she didn't look up at him. And for right now, he was glad, because he was very much afraid that what showed on his face would scare her even more than what she had to be.

"Uncuff her. Now." His words were clipped and quiet, cool, betraying none of the anger burning deep inside him at seeing Shelby sitting there, her arms handcuffed behind the chair.

"She's under arrest. Assault and resisting arrest." Officer Dillon continued to sit there, lounging in the chair across from Shelby, his legs stretched out in front of him. Josh took two more steps forward, stopping less than a foot away, and looked down at him.

"That was a direct order, Officer. Uncuff her. Now."

Dillon finally realized that something wasn't quite right. He straightened in the chair, looking up at Josh as an expression of uncertainty flashed across his face. Josh leaned even closer, and Dillon finally rose from the chair, pushing it back with a screech that echoed in the room. He moved around the table and reached behind Shelby, taking his time in removing the handcuffs. He straightened, shot Josh a resentful scowl, then tossed the cuffs to the table with a loud clang.

Josh stood still, waiting, fixing the officer with his own cool gaze while he watched Shelby from the corner of his eye. She moved her arms to the front and flexed her wrists, then rubbed each hand. Another flash of anger spread through Josh when he saw the indentations on her wrists, caused by cuffs fastened too tightly, for too long. He clenched his jaw but said nothing, waiting for Shelby to look up at him.

But she didn't. She just sat there, rubbing her arms and wrists, her head lowered and her face hid by the fall of her thick hair. Josh counted to ten as the silence stretched around them, and still she didn't look up.

"Are you okay Dr. Martin?" He tried to keep the cold anger from his voice, but she must have sensed it because he could see her stiffen, just the slightest bit. She still didn't look up, just merely nodded. All he wanted to do was kneel by her side and pull her into his arms, reassure her that his anger wasn't directed at her. Surely she knew that. She *must* know that. Josh took a deep breath and said nothing, barely even moved.

"I'd like to know when I can take the perp to Central Booking and begin processing her. Sergeant."

Josh didn't miss the disrespectful sarcasm in Dillon's voice. He fixed the older man with a cold glare, staring until the officer finally shifted and looked away. "There will be no charges filed. She's being released."

"You can't do that! She's under arrest for theft, assaulting a police officer, and resisting arrest. You have no authority here, Sergeant—"

"I'm sure the security tapes that are currently being retrieved will prove the assault and resisting charges are baseless. The theft charges have already been dropped, because there's no basis for them. Dr. Martin has a verified alibi for her whereabouts this weekend."

Dillon began stammering his arguments but Josh ignored them. No, not ignored. He couldn't hear them, not through the red-hot rush of anger that suddenly consumed him when Shelby finally looked up at him.

It wasn't the shocked look in her eyes that caused his anger, or the blotchiness of her normally smooth complexion. It was the mark on her cheek that set him off.

The right side of her face was slightly swollen and beginning to bruise, a faint tinge of red and purple covering her cheekbone. He dropped his gaze lower and saw the marks on her upper arm, a series of fresh bruises in the shape of fingerprints. And there was no doubt in Josh's mind that those fingerprints would match Officer Dillon's.

He rushed forward, pushing Dillon against the wall with both hands, holding him there with one arm across his throat. "What the hell did you do to her?"

"Get off me! I didn't do anything to her!"

Josh ignored him, leaning in even closer, pushing harder against his throat. He wanted to kill the man, to tear him apart with his bare hands for even daring to touch Shelby. "Really? Where did the marks come from? How much police brutality are we going to see on those tapes?"

Dillon's mouth opened and closed but no sound came out. His face was turning an alarming shade of red, and still Josh pushed against him, not caring. Hands closed over his arms and shoulders and he felt himself being pulled away. Words that held no meaning rang in his ears. Several minutes passed before Josh calmed enough to make sense of the mutterings.

His men had come in and pulled him off Dillon, warning him to stop before he went too far. Josh took several long breaths then nodded, letting them know he was fine even though he still wanted to tear into the officer. He took another step back, putting more distance between them before he did exactly that.

"I'm having you put on charges. You can't get away with this!" Dillon's voice came out as a croak as he rubbed his throat, fixing Josh with an angry glare that didn't quite hide his fear.

"With what? We were watching the entire time, we didn't see anything."

"Didn't see a thing."

"Then I'll get the tapes to prove—"

"Oh, didn't anyone tell you? There's been a malfunction. The camera in this room doesn't work." Johnson delivered the final blow with a small smile that didn't reach his eyes.

"But the tapes from the museum...those are a different story. The Lieutenant's already looked at them, and he doesn't seem too happy. I think, though, that if you leave now, he may just forget about looking for you."

Dillon looked at each of them, at Josh and his men, his eyes bulging in shock and his mouth sputtering in outrage. Josh took a menacing step toward him and the man finally moved, pushing around them and rushing through the door.

Johnson clapped Josh on the shoulder then led everyone else out of the room, pulling the door closed behind them. Josh clasped his hands behind his neck and closed his eyes, taking deep breaths to calm the fury that still raged inside him. He worried that it would bubble to the surface again as soon as he looked at Shelby and saw the marks marring her smooth skin.

In as much control as he could manage, he finally opened his eyes and turned to face her. She hadn't moved at all, as far as he could tell. She still sat rigid at the table, her head lowered, her face covered by her hair. Josh closed the distance between them and knelt down next to her, gently reaching out and pushing her hair behind her ear.

She flinched but still didn't look at him. Josh took another deep breath and lowered his hand along her arm, feeling the cold dampness of her skin against his palm. He grabbed her hand and held it, inwardly wincing at the trembling in her fingers.

"Are you okay?"

She shook her head but said nothing, still wouldn't look at him. Josh watched her for a few long seconds, then did what he had wanted to do as soon as he had walked in. He reached out for her and pulled her into his arms, holding her tight against the warmth of his body. She held herself stiffly at first, then slowly leaned into him. Her arms came around his neck and she clung to him. Josh felt her shoulders heave and the breath hitched in his chest when he felt her warm tears against his neck. And he just held her, rubbing her back with one hand, unable to squeeze words past his tight throat.

They stayed that way for long minutes, until Josh lost all track of time. She finally shifted in his arms, pulling back the tiniest bit. He eased his hold on her and stood up, pulling her up with him. She still wouldn't look at him, so he cupped her chin in one hand and gently tilted her face toward him. But she kept her gaze lowered, still not looking at him.

Josh swallowed his sigh and leaned forward, gently kissing her bruised cheek. He wrapped one arm around her shoulder and led her out of the room.

"C'mon Shelby. Let's go home."

Chapter Seventeen

Josh glanced over at Shelby, his hand tightening on the steering wheel. She had yet to say anything to him, not a single word. And she wouldn't look at him, either. She kept her head lowered, the curtain of her hair hiding her face as she kept rubbing at her wrists.

Josh clenched his jaw tight against the raw fury that wanted to break free at the sight of those wrists. Her flesh no longer bore the indentations of the cuffs, but discoloration mottled the skin where they had been. He swore if he ever saw Dillon again...

He shook the thought off, knowing his anger wouldn't help. The lieutenant was investigating. Josh would have to settle for that, at least for now.

Because right now, his concern was for Shelby.

Her silence was unnatural and her dazed look worried him. He wondered if she was in some kind of shock.

Hell, she deserved to be in shock. Things like being subjected to police brutality and being arrested didn't happen to people like her. Part of him felt guilty for bringing the darker side of humanity into her life, which was irrational.

He was just thankful he had been able to stop it before it was too late. Knowing what she had already been through, it would have been worse if she had been taken to Central Booking. So much worse.

Josh ran his hand through his hair, not surprised to see that his own fingers shook slightly. From anger, from worry. From a sense of helplessness that was foreign to him. He took a deep breath and looked back over at Shelby. From what he could tell, she still hadn't moved. She just kept looking down in her lap, her hands rubbing her wrists over and over.

Josh changed lanes so quickly that cars behind him blew their horns. He ignored them, intent only on getting Shelby home. To his place. He had originally planned on taking her to her own apartment, but he changed his mind. It made more sense to take her to his place. His place was closer. He could better protect her there.

Protect. Where the hell had that word come from? Guilt immediately followed that thought. Protect her? He hadn't done a very good job of that so far.

He pulled into his development a few minutes later, coming to a stop in front of his townhouse. He expected Shelby to look over at him, to at least question where they were. But she still didn't move.

Worry ramped up his pulse, chasing away the anger. Josh got out of the car and hurried around to the other side, quickly opening the door and tugging on her hand to help her out. She winced at the touch and he cursed himself for hurting her more.

Yet she still said nothing, just followed him quietly to the front door and inside. He yanked off his jacket and tossed it on the coat rack in the entranceway then locked the door and stood there, not sure what to do next.

He had some brandy in the liquor cabinet. Maybe that would help. He looked over at her, ready to tell her he was going to get her something to drink when the words died in his throat.

Shelby was standing in the entranceway, her face pale, her hair disheveled, shaking. Not just shivering, but shaking so hard he could hear her teeth chattering. Josh forgot all about the brandy and picked her up, cradling her in his arms then carrying her upstairs. He thought that if he could just get her warm, she would be okay. If he could just get her warm...

He carried her through his bedroom and into the master bath, then gently set her on her feet. When he was sure she wouldn't fall, that she could still stand, he stepped away from her and reached into the large glass shower stall and turned on the water. He undid his holster and pulled it off, carefully placing it out of the way in the bathroom closet.

Then he moved in front of Shelby and reached for her chin, tilting her head back so she could see him.

"Shelby. Sweetheart, talk to me." She blinked at him but still said nothing. He clenched his jaw and began unbuttoning her blouse, thinking again that if he could just get her warm, she would be fine.

Steam floated from the shower stall and sweat broke out on his forehead from the moist heat, but Shelby was still shaking. He fumbled with the last few buttons of her blouse, then eased it over her shoulders and down her arms, mindful of her bruises.

Then he sucked in his breath, his heart lurching at the sight of another bruise, a large one on her left side, along her ribcage. He swore softly and clenched his jaw against the warring emotions turning him inside out: anger, guilt, fury. And above them all, an overwhelming need to protect.

He pushed them all away, focusing only on Shelby and her shivering, and the need to get her warm. He reached behind her and unhooked her bra, then eased that off her as well before gently turning her around so he could unbutton her skirt.

Yet another bruise marred her skin, a round one in the low center of her back, the kind of bruise that was made by a knee being forced into someone's back.

"I'm going to fucking kill him." The words escaped in a growl before he could think to stop them, and he thought Shelby flinched. But he couldn't be sure, because she was shivering even more now.

Josh pushed her skirt down her hips and turned her around, then picked her up and stepped into the shower with her, testing the water temperature with his own body before moving her under the gentle spray. He closed his eyes and rested his cheek against the top of her head, letting the water flow over them, praying she would stop shivering, hoping this worked. "Shelby, sweetheart, please. You're starting to scare me. Tell me what you need. Say something. Anything."

Long minutes went by, and still he held her under the spray, waiting, his heart pounding in his chest as her body continued to shake in his arms. Water rolled down his face as the misting steam surrounded them, wrapping them in a moist blanket of pale intimacy. Josh took a deep breath and held it, wondering if he was imagining things or if her shivering had slowed.

And then she spoke.

The words were nothing more than a whisper, lost

in the swirling steam and spraying water. But the sound of her voice nearly caused his legs to buckle in relief, and he leaned against the wall for support. He took a deep breath and let it out in a rush, then lowered his head even closer to hear her.

"What? I didn't—"

"Shoes. You still have your shoes on."

Josh laughed, except it came out as a strangled choke of relief that he had to swallow back. Shelby's head relaxed against his shoulder, her hand coming up to rest high on his chest. He tightened his arms around her and just held her, his eyes closed as relief washed over him.

Another minute passed by in silence then Shelby wriggled out of his arms, slowly lowering her legs until she was standing. Josh kept his hands on her arms, supporting her until he was certain she wouldn't fall. She stood still, the water falling over her head and shoulders, before finally tilting her head up at him.

The look in her eyes—lost and sorrowful—acted like a powerful blow to his gut. He would do anything—anything—to make that look go away, to bring a sparkle of life back into her beautiful eyes.

Josh reached up to undo his necktie, yanking it off and tossing it out of the shower before unbuttoning the top button of his shirt. Then he reached behind him for the shower gel and squirted some into his hands, working it into a thick lather before running his hands along her shoulders and arms, washing her.

His hands glided gently over her bruises, taking special care with them, and he wished he could wash them away, that the water would rinse them off her body as cleanly as it rinsed the lather from her skin. He trailed his hands back to her shoulders, his fingers pressing gently into the bunched muscles of her neck, kneading. Shelby's eyes closed and her head tilted back the tiniest bit as he worked on the knots.

"Turn around." His voice was hoarse and he chalked it up to the steam and water surrounding them. She did as he asked, her head leaning forward now. He pushed the hair away from her neck and squeezed more gel into his hands, then worked it over her back. He watched her body's reaction to each place he touched, focusing his fingers on the knots in her shoulders and neck before moving to her lower back.

He reached the bruise, tracing it lightly with his hands, and clenched his jaw when she stiffened under his touch. He took several deep breaths, in and out, forcing himself to calm. Then he leaned down and trailed his lips lightly along the bruise on her back, wishing he could kiss all the bruises away, wishing he could kiss her pains away.

He reached for her left wrist and held it between his hands, rubbing the marks that circled it. Shelby stiffened and pulled her wrist away, cradling it in front of her where he couldn't see it.

"I'm sorry."

The words floored him—because they came from Shelby before he had a chance to utter them himself. He straightened and slowly turned her around to face him, tilting her head up with a finger on her chin.

"Sorry? Shelby, my God, you have nothing to be sorry for!"

"I didn't want to get you in trouble. And now..." She closed her eyes, refusing to look at him. She was worried about him? Josh's heart squeezed tight against his chest and he had to swallow several times before speaking.

"Shelby, you did nothing wrong. Nothing. Do you hear me? Open your eyes, look at me." He cupped his palm against her cheek and rubbed her lower lip with his thumb, waiting for her eyes to open, waiting for her to look at him.

"You did nothing wrong. *You* are the victim here. And seeing what that asshole did to you..." Josh swallowed against the emotion clogging his throat and filling his words. He took another deep breath, searching for at least a surface calm, not wanting to scare Shelby. "The only person in trouble here is him. Not me. Certainly not you. You did nothing wrong, so stop thinking that you did."

Shelby's eyes searched his, like she was trying to decide if she should believe him or not. He continued stroking her lower lip with his thumb, his gaze holding hers, using his own eyes to convince her of the truth.

"I've never been arrested before. I didn't like it." Her voice was quiet and so matter-of-fact that Josh laughed, a strangled sound he couldn't keep from escaping. He pulled her into his arms and held her tight against him for a long minute, then stepped back just enough so he could claim her mouth in a gentle kiss.

"Sweetheart, nobody likes getting arrested. That's why it's only supposed to be for criminals." His eyes drifted to the bruise on her cheek and he clenched his jaw again. "I could kill him for what he did to you."

Something of his intent must have shown on his face because Shelby quickly shook her head. She reached up and covered his mouth with her hand, her eyes serious. "Josh, no. Please. He didn't..." She motioned to the bruise on her cheek and side with her free hand and shook her head again. "I tripped and fell on top of my bag. That's how—"

He reached up and moved her hand away from his mouth, moving it so her bruised and marked wrist was between them. "Bullshit. This doesn't happen from tripping." He reached behind her with his free hand and gently traced the bruise on her lower back. "This doesn't happen from tripping. This is from a cop who's gone too far. And when I think about what he did to you..."

"Then don't think about it, Josh. Please. I don't want you to get into any more trouble."

"Shelby, I'm not in trouble—"

"Please Josh."

He closed his mouth against the additional reassurances he wanted to make. For some reason, she honestly thought he was either in trouble for something, or would get into trouble for something. So he just nodded, which seemed to be all the reassurance she was looking for.

He reached up and brushed her wet hair away from her face, studying her, looking for left-over signs of the shock she had been in earlier. The terrifyingly blank stare was gone from her eyes, and her shivering seemed to have completely stopped. Josh reached around her and turned the faucet handle, adding some more hot water to the spray that still fell on them.

He placed a quick kiss on her mouth then stepped away. "There's still plenty of hot water left. Take your time washing up, and I'll go make us some lunch."

He had one foot out of the glass shower stall when her hand tightened around his arm, stopping him. Josh turned, thinking she needed something, and froze at the look on her face.

Her expression was shy, but fiercely determined at the same time. She chewed on her lower lip and looked up at him, uncertainty mingling with the small spark in her eyes. "Stay here with me. Please."

It came out as a statement, but Josh didn't miss the question under the words. He stilled, afraid to move, wondering what to do. The rational part of his brain said she probably needed time alone, time to rant or cry or...or something...in private.

But her hand tightened around his arm and she pulled him back into the shower, and the rational part of his brain was overpowered by the sudden intensity of his body's reaction. He let her pull him closer, afraid to move on his own, worried that he misunderstood her intent.

No, he didn't think he misunderstood. Because she stepped toward him, pressing her body against his, closing her mouth over his in a warm, tentative kiss. His arms immediately came around her, holding her closer. He lifted his head and looked down at her, his rational brain striving for command over his body before he did something completely stupid.

"Are you sure?"

She met his gaze with her own steady one and nodded, all uncertainty gone from her eyes. Her hands came between them and fumbled with the buttons of his shirt, struggling to work the round disks through the stiff, water-soaked material.

She muttered something that sounded suspiciously like a curse under her breath as she continued her struggle with the first button. Josh smiled at the fierce look of determination on her face and gently moved her hands away. The shirt was ruined anyway, not that he would let her know that. He reached up and ripped the shirt open, popping the buttons off with a damp tearing sound.

Shelby's eyes widened in surprise, then she smiled and looked up at him, running her hands along his wet chest as he struggled to pull his arms out of the sopping shirt.

And Josh quickly realized that everything he had ever heard about undressing in a shower was a complete lie. There was nothing easy, graceful, or even remotely sexy about struggling to peel out of wet clothes while standing under running water. His struggles were made even more difficult because Shelby had found the shower gel and insisted on lathering it over each body part he finally freed from his clothes. Their laughter—Shelby was laughing, thank God—mixed together with the steam and floated around them as he hopped around, trying to get out of his shoes and pants at the same time.

Until, finally, every last piece of clothing had been discarded, tossed into a sopping pile on the bathroom floor. Josh straightened, out of breath, and smiled at Shelby. His laughter died instantly at the look on her face, at the desire and raw need so clear in her eyes as she looked up at him.

He reached for her, his hands cupping her face as he slanted his mouth over hers in a fierce kiss before running his mouth along her jaw and throat. He lost himself even as he claimed her, with his lips, his tongue, his touch.

Shelby's hands ran along his shoulders and chest, lower, her touch hot against his slick skin. She reached between them and wrapped her hand around his cock, her fingers closing firmly over him. She squeezed, stroking him from base to tip, base to tip. Josh clenched his jaw at the sensation, his cock growing even harder at her touch.

His breath left him in a rush when Shelby shifted, wrapping one leg high around him. She rubbed the tip of his cock against her, letting him feel her slick heat, so different from the warm water splashing over them.

"I need you inside me, Josh. Now." Her whispered plea broke something inside him. He opened his eyes and looked down at her, at the desire in her gaze as she stared up at him.

Needing him.

Trusting him.

Josh grabbed her hips and lifted, turning to brace her against the cool tile of the wall as he drove into her with one hard thrust of his hips. Her legs wrapped high and tight around his waist, opening herself more fully to him as her head fell back. He thrust again, her fingers digging into her hips, holding her against him, her tight sheath welcoming him.

He thrust again and again, losing himself in her heat as he buried himself to the hilt. Over and over, his hips pumping, driving himself deeper. Her lips parted slightly and her moans grew louder with each of his thrusts. Her hips pushed forward, meeting his, following his rhythm.

He spread his legs for better balance and wrapped one arm under her, supporting her as he continued to thrust, his rhythm increasing, getting faster. Her slick heat covered him and her muscles clenched around him, pulling him even deeper inside.

His thrusts became faster, desperate, as she tightened around him. She screamed his name as her orgasm exploded. Her muscles quivered around his cock and the slick wetness of her cum coated his hard length as she rocked against him, her breathing harsh in his ear.

Josh exploded inside her, the violent strength of his climax shattering him as he filled her. He continued driving into her, hearing her call his name over and over, feeling her sheath tighten and convulse around him one more time.

He slowed his thrusts and lowered his head, closing his mouth over Shelby's and swallowing her soft cries. He gentled the kiss as her body slowly relaxed against his, as her muscles unclenched and eased. The heat of their mingled sex flowed over him, covering him, filling him with a savage possession that he tried to tamp down.

And still he kissed her, claiming her. Possessing her even as he waited for guilt and recrimination to claim him.

But neither did. Instead, he was filled with a sense of peace. Of belonging. He broke the kiss and gently pulled away, looking down into Shelby's eyes, wondering if she knew, if she could feel it, too.

Her steady gaze pierced him, filled with the same bewilderment he felt. Bewilderment, then the realization that they had just had unprotected sex. Josh held his breath, waiting for her reaction. Something unspoken passed between them, something he refused to give voice to or try to define.

And then she smiled. Hesitant at first, until it grew and drew him in. Josh answered her smile with his own, then gently lowered her to her feet, his gaze holding hers steady.

They finished showering without spoken words, their touches slow against each other until the water finally cooled. Josh helped her from the shower and dried her off, then wrapped her in an oversized towel.

Still not speaking, still not needing words between

them, he led her out of the bathroom and over to his bed. He pulled back the covers and climbed in, pulling her down beside him. He covered them both with a sheet, tucking her close against his side.

Shelby smiled up at him and pressed a slow sweet kiss against his lips. Then she rolled onto her side and settled against him, taking his hands in hers and curling them against the beat of her heart.

Josh listened as her breathing evened out, holding her as she drifted off to sleep. He stayed that way for a long time, contentment warming him as his own eyes finally drifted close and he followed her in slumber.

Chapter Eighteen

Josh looked so bewildered and lost that Shelby almost felt sorry for him. Almost. But she didn't because the entire thing was his idea and, therefore, his fault.

She doubted if he'd see it that way, though, so she chose to stay quiet, merely smiling over at him. He stood at the doorway of the living room, his hands on his hips, his dark eyes narrowed at her, like he knew exactly what she was thinking.

He finally shook his head and muttered under his breath, then strode into the room and leaned over her. He cupped his hands around her face and kissed her, a deep, thorough, soul-stealing kiss that curled her toes and left her breathless when he finally pulled away.

"Just relax and don't overdo it today. And get plenty of rest for tonight when I get home. You're going to need it." He placed another kiss on her lips then turned and walked away.

The other two women in the room followed him with their eyes, their mouths open in surprise until he closed the front door with a click. Then they turned and looked at her, their smiles and laughter filling the room.

"Oh...my...God! He is so hot, and I am so jealous!" Amanda leaned back against the overstuffed chair and fanned her face. Chrissy looked at both of them and rolled her eyes, her smile fading as she shook her head.

"Shelby, you're the only person I know who can turn a one-night stand into a relationship."

Shelby looked over at Chrissy, not sure what to make of her words. She waited, sure that something caustic and sarcastic would follow, but Chrissy merely watched her. A long minute went by before she leaned forward, excitement in her eyes. "So come on, tell us the details. You're in love with him, aren't you?"

"What? No. No, of course not." Shelby shook her head in stern denial, her face heating under their scrutiny. And she could tell from the looks in their eyes that neither one of them believed her. She shook her head again and said out loud what she had been telling herself. "It's too soon. We haven't been together that long. I can't be in love with him."

Amanda and Chrissy exchanged knowing looks with each other, but neither said anything. And Shelby knew she hadn't convinced either one of them—anymore than she had convinced herself. So she repeated the words again, enunciating each one clearly.

"I am not in love with Josh. I can't be." Her stomach rolled at the words, creating a hollow pit deep inside that left her feeling empty.

"Say what you want, but I don't believe you."

"Neither do I. And judging from what I saw before he left, he's certainly in love with you." Chrissy's voice was matter-of-fact, causing Shelby to look up at her sharply. A spark of hope flared inside her and she tamped it down, refusing to encourage it, refusing to think about it. Refusing to acknowledge it.

"Yeah, and you're such an expert at love!" Amanda laughed, taking the sting from her words, but Chrissy only smiled, her eyes holding Shelby's.

She looked away from both of their knowing glances, her gaze falling to her folded hands and the ring of bruises that circled each wrist.

A week had gone by since her 'arrest' and some of the nightmarish details were still hazy in her memory. The one thing that she recalled with precision clarity was Josh's reaction—and his defense of her. She had been so afraid that she would be guilty in his eyes. Never mind that she was innocent, never mind that her fear was irrational, with no basis other than a shallow comparison to her few-and-far-between past relationships. She knew that, but the fear had still been there.

Which only made his fierce reaction and defense of her that much more surprising. That didn't mean he loved her. He was a man of honor and integrity; she had learned that about him almost immediately. So of course he would rush to her defense, in spite of her irrational fear that he would believe the worst.

But that didn't mean he loved her.

"So are you going to tell us exactly what happened?"

Shelby looked up, surprised to see Chrissy and Amanda closely watching her. She touched her still-bruised cheek with one hand, embarrassed even though she did nothing wrong.

"I told you, there was a misunderstanding and I was arrested, but the charges got dropped."

"No, Shelby. That was a summary, not details. We want details."

"Every detail. Because the Shelby we know would never have even come close to doing anything to get arrested for!"

"That's just it, I didn't do anything." Shelby shifted on the sofa, tucking her legs more comfortably under her. She looked from Chrissy to Amanda and back again, then let out a heavy sigh, knowing neither one of them would be happy until they heard the entire story.

So she gave it to them, every little detail she could remember. Their reaction was nothing less than she expected of her friends, and by the time she was finished, she knew that Josh had been elevated to hero-status in their eyes.

"My God, Shelby. That's awful. I can't even imagine going through all that." Amanda shook her head, her sympathy clear in her eyes. Shelby didn't know how to reply, knowing that the experience was much worse than the telling. She didn't want to remember going through it, didn't want to recall the details, especially since she now knew it *could* have been worse. So much worse, if not for Josh's interference.

"I can't believe David just stood there and let that cop do that." Chrissy's sympathy was tempered by her outrage. "Actually, yes I can. He always was a complete piece of shit. I never did understand what you saw in him. I think you should get even with him when you go back to work. Do something really awful, like...I don't know what. Give me a few minutes and I'll think of something."

"I'm not going back to work."

Silence greeted Shelby's quiet statement. Both

women looked at her in astonishment for so long that Shelby finally looked away, dropping her gaze back to her lap. The silence stretched on, until Chrissy finally found her voice again.

"Why the hell not? You're not going to let this get in your way, are you? You love that job!"

Shelby took a deep breath and shook her head, then finally looked back at her friends. "I got fired."

"What?"

"When?"

"David called yesterday and left a message on my voicemail. It seems that the Board of Directors isn't interested in having someone of my 'questionable character' working for the museum. So," Shelby swallowed around the thickness in her throat and shrugged. "I'm apparently out of a job."

"They can't do that!" Chrissy's voice was nearly a shriek in the surrounding quiet. She half-stood, then flopped back down in the chair and looked over at Amanda. "They can't do that, can they?"

"No, of course not. I mean, I don't think they can. Shelby, don't you have a contract?"

Shelby pulled the throw pillow into her lap and fingered the corner of it, her brow furrowed in concentration. "Yes, to I think they can, because they did. And yes to the contract. But I don't think it matters because there's an out-clause in there. Something about conduct and professionalism. Which doesn't matter anyway, because it was time for my review. I was hoping to get that promotion but now...I guess not."

"Promotion? What promotion? You didn't tell us anything about any promotion."

"Because there wasn't anything to tell. I would have been doing pretty much the same exact thing with a few added responsibilities but my title would have changed. Guess it doesn't matter now, though, does it?"

"It does matter!" Chrissy's indignation was increasing, and Shelby fought back a smile at the realization that her friend's anger was on her behalf. Yes, Chrissy could be a real bitch...but it was nice when she was that way *for* you instead of *to* you. "There's got to be a way to fight this. I mean, sure, I never understood why you get all excited about all that dusty old stuff, but it's what you love doing! I can't believe David just fired you. There has to be a way to fight this. Tell her, Amanda."

"I don't know. I need to think about it. It seems like there should be, though. Shelby, do you think it would be worth having a meeting with David? Maybe talk face-to-face and see—"

"No, absolutely not. I don't even want to be in the same room with him. There's something different about him." Shelby studied her two friends, wondering if she should tell them what she thought. The old Shelby would have kept her suspicions to herself, afraid of saying anything, afraid of calling attention to herself. But the new Shelby...the new Shelby was learning to speak her mind, to act on instinct instead of questioning it. The new Shelby was no longer content to just sit by the sidelines, not anymore.

Chrissy and Amanda both looked at her expectantly, waiting. So the new Shelby took a deep breath and told them what she suspected.

"I think he's the one who took the artifacts. And I think he's the one who put them in my office. I think he did it to have me fired, and I don't know why."

Silence greeted her words, and the new Shelby

almost regretted saying them out loud. But she shook her head and straightened, feeling the rightness of her suspicions, even more now that she had verbalized them. She couldn't prove anything, but her instincts screamed that she was right.

"Shelby, are you sure?" Amanda finally asked. There was no judgment in her gaze, no doubt, just conviction of friendship. Shelby looked over at Chrissy and saw the same unwavering support in her eyes.

The strength of her conviction grew and she nodded, more sure now than before. "I'm sure. I can't prove anything, and I don't know why, but I know, deep down, he did it."

"What did Josh say when you told him?"

Shelby looked over at Chrissy, not surprised that the question came from her, now that Josh had achieved hero-status in her eyes. Shelby shrugged and looked away, not able to meet her friend's gaze.

"I haven't really talked to him about it. I haven't even told him I got fired yet."

Chrissy and Amanda both looked at her in shock, the disbelief clear in their eyes as they stared at her.

"What?"

"Shelby! Why haven't you told him? You need to tell him." Certainty rang clear in Amanda's voice as she spoke. Shelby looked at both of them, then slowly shook her head. She shouldn't have said anything, knowing this was how they would react.

"I can't. If I do, Josh will go after him, and then he'll get in trouble. I can't let him get in trouble over this."

"But Shelby, he's a cop. He'll know what to do."

"And it's not like he can get in trouble for doing his job."

"That's just it. He wouldn't be doing it because of his job. He'd be doing it for me. And he really doesn't like David. I mean, he *really* doesn't like him."

"Which only proves he has great sense."

"Chrissy!"

"What?" She gave Amanda a defiant look, then turned back to Shelby. "You have to tell him."

Shelby sunk back into the overstuffed cushions, suddenly tired and even more confused. Part of her knew her friends were right—she needed to tell Josh her suspicions. But that's all they were: suspicions. She knew, with absolute certainty, that if she said anything to Josh, he would go after David. And then he would get into trouble, because he'd be doing it for her, not because it was his job.

She shook her head again, adamant. She would not let Josh get into trouble. "I can't tell him, not without any proof. If I had proof, it would be different. But I don't. It's just a gut feeling."

Forlorn silence settled over the three of them, stretching around them as they watched each other. Chrissy finally straightened, a small smile teasing her pursed lips. Shelby felt her stomach roll at the look on Chrissy's face. A glance at Amanda let her know that she felt the same sudden dread. But Chrissy spoke before either one of them could say anything.

"So then let's get proof."

"No! Absolutely not! Chrissy—"

Shelby spoke over Amanda, interrupting her even though she was tempted to say the same thing. Instead she fixed Chrissy with a thoughtful gaze. "And how would we do that? If the police haven't been able to find anything, how would we?"

"I don't know. Maybe you could just ask him. If it

was just the two of you, maybe he'd gloat or say something stupid. You could carry a tape recorder or something."

"Oh, for crying out loud Chrissy. You watch too much television. Do you honestly think he would just come out and tell Shelby something like that? He's not stupid."

"No. But he thinks everyone else is stupid. And he's arrogant." The words hung between them and they all shared a knowing look. Amanda finally sat back and shook her head once, a quick jerky movement as she folded her arms across her chest.

"Both of you are crazy if you think this would work."

Shelby straightened, lowering her feet to the floor and leaning forward. "Maybe, but what if it *does* work?"

"No."

Chrissy turned away from Amanda, ignoring her. "When you said David called and left a voice mail, telling you that you were fired...did you talk to him at all?"

"No, it was just the voice mail."

"So you didn't call him back?"

"No."

"Shelby! He left a message saying you were fired and you didn't even call him back?"

Chrissy waved away Amanda's outburst with a quick flick of her hand. "No, that's perfect. Since you never actually talked to him, you don't really *know* you're fired, right? So nobody could say anything about you being there."

Shelby studied Chrissy, her mind running through the different possibilities. Put that way, she conceded that maybe, just maybe...it might work. She refused to think of everything that could wrong.

"And what is she going to do if someone confronts her and tells her to get out?"

Chrissy shrugged. "So what if they do? She can claim she doesn't know anything, and then say she wants to see David. That would be even better."

Amanda and Shelby both stared at Chrissy. She looked first at one then at the other, and shrugged. "What?"

"I knew you were sneaky, but I didn't know how sneaky."

Chrissy waved away the remark and shrugged again. "Please. This isn't that sneaky. In fact, it's pretty tame. So when are we going to do this? I don't think we should wait too much longer, or else it might look funny, suddenly showing up."

"We?"

"Of course, 'we'." Amanda jumped in. "I still think it's crazy and that something could go wrong, but you don't think we'd let you do it by yourself, do you?"

"I don't know. I didn't think—"

"Yeah, yeah. Whatever. Okay, I think we should set this up for tomorrow. That way we can get everything we need, and make sure we have all the details worked out." Chrissy slid off the chair and moved to the floor in front of the sofa, quickly followed by Amanda, who was already pulling a pad of paper from her bag. The three of them huddled together, fine-tuning the hare-brained idea.

By the time they were finished, Shelby thought that maybe, just maybe, they might be able to pull it off.

She hoped.

Chapter Nineteen

Weariness seeped through Josh as he dragged himself out of the car. It had been a long day—a day of chasing leads and coming up empty, and not just with the latest vice operation. He met with Special Agent Levins and they both reviewed the historical society's surveillance tape—or lack of it. Both men thought it more than coincidence that both of the tapes that might contain much needed evidence were conveniently corrupted or blank. They shared their suspicions, some more possible than others, all of them pointing to Dr. David Spear.

But in the end, that's all they were: suspicions. They had no proof. They had no motive. Without either of those things—or even better, a witnessed confession—it was over.

The property had been returned.

Josh suppressed a shudder when he remembered seeing it. A lock of President Lincoln's hair from his autopsy. There was something obscenely morbid about that. He still didn't know who in their right minds would consider that historically significant, let alone think it was worth stealing.

But who was he to judge other people's obsessions?

He rolled his head, working out the kinks in his neck as he let himself in the door. As soon as he crossed the threshold, he vowed to put work out of his mind. All he wanted to do was pull Shelby into his arms, preferably naked, and hold her.

His cock twitched at the thought of her naked body in his arms, and he smiled. Okay, so maybe he wanted to do more than hold her. That would certainly go a long way to getting his mind off work and improving his mood.

But the house was quiet when he walked through the door. Too quiet. It reminded him of the silence of a vacant house, a sound he was used to from years of living by himself.

A sound that opened a hollowness in his gut. A sound he no longer enjoyed, not after having Shelby stay with him these past few days.

Josh paused in the entranceway, his head cocked to the side, listening. A frown creased his forehead as he tossed his keys on the side table then shrugged out of his jacket. He hung it in the hall closet then continued into the house, surprised by the silence, wondering where Shelby was. A split second of irrational fear that she left, that she was no longer here, gripped him.

He walked further into the living room then stopped.

Shelby was curled up on the sofa, one hand tucked under her chin, sound asleep. The wild tangle of her hair framed the peaceful features of her face, hiding the bruise that marred her skin. The hollowness that threatened to swallow him only seconds before disappeared, to be replaced by contradicting feelings of anger and possessiveness.

He pushed the anger at what she had endured away, and was tempted to do the same to the possessiveness. But he was too honest with himself to ignore it. Hell yeah, he was possessive. Shelby was his. And he knew himself better than to kid himself into thinking this was just some weird temporary feeling. If the emptiness that had threatened him at the thought of Shelby being gone hadn't opened his eyes, then the other emotions would have. The quick surge of remaining anger over someone hurting her coupled with this powerful sense of possessiveness were too strong to ignore.

The emotions and realizations coming so closely together, one on top the other on top the other, drove into him with a force strong enough to make his knees go weak. No, this wasn't a temporary thing he was feeling. And this wasn't a temporary thing he wanted.

Not with Shelby.

He took a deep breath and held it, waiting for the rational part of his mind to argue. No argument appeared, and he slowly let his breath out.

And realized that instead of being anxious or even disbelieving, he felt...calm. Accepting.

Josh shook his head and walked deeper into the living room, keeping his steps light and quiet so he wouldn't disturb Shelby. She must have sensed his presence, even in her sleep, because her eyes fluttered open, meeting his own gaze with a sleepy honest emotion.

Josh swallowed at the sight of that unguarded look

then offered her a small smile as she blinked, effectively hiding the open emotion he had seen in her eyes so briefly, yet so clearly.

But it was too late, because Josh had seen it. And he realized that both of them were playing games with each other. With themselves. He smiled again and lowered himself to the sofa, not surprised when Shelby scooted over enough to give him room before he even moved.

He watched her, his eyes taking in every detail: the wayward strand of hair that clung to her cheek, the slight wrinkles in the soft cotton night shirt where it twisted around her waist, the plump fullness of her lips, still soft and lush from sleep. He leaned forward and dropped a lingering kiss on her mouth, feeling the warmth of her tiny sigh against his own lips as he slowly pulled away.

For the briefest of seconds, he thought about telling her how he felt. Or at least, how he thought he felt. But instead he straightened and offered her a small smile as her fingers twined with his. "You should have gone up to bed instead of waiting down here for me. It would have been more comfortable for you."

"No, I'm fine. I didn't mean to fall asleep." Shelby propped herself up on one elbow and looked around, still blinking. "What time is it?"

"Almost eight o'clock."

"What?" She gave him a bewildered look, then glanced around with a frown. "At night, or morning?"

Josh laughed at the expression on her face, still soft with sleep even as confusion crossed her features. He squeezed her fingers and leaned down to give her another quick kiss. "At night. You must have had a wild day, huh?"

"What? Oh, no. Not really." Shelby pulled her hand from his and pushed herself up to a sitting position. She ran one hand through her hair, pushing it out of her face, then rubbed her eyes and blinked some more. "What about you? Did you have a wild day?"

"No, I can honestly say today was a boring, uneventful, disappointing day."

"Why disappointing?"

"Because your case is doomed to be filed away as 'unsolved'. There are no viable suspects, and since everything was returned, there's no reason to keep investigating."

"What? That's not right! Why not?"

"It comes down to money and budgets. Nobody has money to waste when the property is already recovered. Maybe something will turn up eventually, but it's no longer a priority. Not for the Feds, not for us." He leaned down and kissed the frown that creased her forehead. "Try not to let it bother you too much. So, what else did you do today?"

"I, um...I got a few things from my place and brought them over. Just a few things. I wasn't sure...I mean, I didn't think you'd mind but...I can take them back..."

Shelby looked away, a faint blush turning her cheeks pink. Josh reached out and cupped her face in both hands, turning her head so she faced him. He waited until she looked at him, really looked at him, his gaze steady on hers until understanding—and surprise—flared in the green and gold depths of her eyes. Then he lowered his head and claimed her mouth in a powerful kiss. His tongue swept across her lips, demanding she open to him, then plunged inside, intent on plundering, conquering, claiming.

Her body surrendered to his, creating his own surrender in turn. He slanted his mouth more fully over hers, his hands tightening on her face and tilting her head back as his tongue plunged deeper into the warm recesses of her mouth. He felt her hands come up to rest on his chest, felt his shirt twist in one of her fists as she leaned more fully into him.

Josh eased her onto her back, the weight of his upper body pushing her into the overstuffed cushions as he stretched out, half on top of her. This was ridiculous, making out on the sofa like a teenager trying to get to third base. A king size bed waited for them upstairs. All Josh had to do was pull back, to take her hand and lead her upstairs...

But he didn't want to wait. He wanted her with a consuming hunger he couldn't explain. He wanted her. Now.

Josh pulled his mouth from hers, dragging his lips along her jaw to her throat, down to her neck where he bit lightly. Shelby arched against him, her head falling back, her breath harsh in his ear. He ran his hand along her throat, down to her chest, palming the hard peak of her nipple through the thin cotton of her shirt. He replaced his touch with his mouth, teasing her with his tongue as he skimmed his hand down along her side and grabbed the hem of her shirt, pushing it up until even that slight barrier between them was gone.

He pulled the tight peak of one nipple into his mouth, sucking and tasting. His hand skimmed along her side, down further to her hips, where he reached under the edge of her lacy thong and found heaven in the searing dampness between her legs.

Shelby fisted her hands in his hair as she arched against him, her hips tilting up as he teased her damp clit. He slid two fingers inside her, feeling her muscles clench around him, pulling him in deeper, teasing him in return.

"I need you inside me, Josh. Please." Shelby's hoarse plea ripped through him, dragging a groan from him. He pulled back and looked down at her, at the need on her face. He groaned again and tore at his own clothes, all thoughts of wooing and romance and foreplay gone from his head. He grabbed for his wallet and pulled a condom out, sheathing himself with it as Shelby pulled her sleep shirt off.

Then he was stretched out on top of her, her legs wrapping high around his waist as he plunged into her with one hard thrust. He eased out of her, then thrust again, burying himself deep inside her welcoming heat. Again. And again.

There was nothing gentle about their lovemaking. No, this was a possession, a claiming. For both of them. Because she wouldn't let him gentle his pace, refused to let him hold back. Instead, she met each of his thrusts with her own, demanding he hold nothing back, giving the same until her body arched and tightened, then shattered around him.

And still she refused to let Josh hold back, urging him deeper inside her with her body, her demanding words. Josh wrapped one arm under her, tilting her hips, and plunged deeper, deeper still until his name was ripped from her lips in a hoarse scream as she shattered again. He plunged one final time, feeling his own body tighten with his release with a driving force that left him breathless.

He held himself over her, almost afraid to move as her muscles continued squeezing him, the pleasure so sharp it was nearly painful. When he was finally able to move, it was only enough to lower himself more fully on top of her, to tuck her against him as he held her, their bodies melded together as one.

She whispered in his ear, the words so soft he knew instinctively that she didn't mean for him to hear. His arms tightened around her as he turned his head, pressing his own lips against her temple and mouthing the words he wasn't quite ready to say out loud.

I love you, too.

Chapter Twenty

"I never thought I'd say this, but those boots are so you!"

Shelby glanced down at her feet then looked back up at Chrissy, not able to hide her smile. "Aren't they great? Josh bought them for me for when we go out on his motorcycle."

Amanda shook her head and pushed in front of Chrissy. "Yeah, they're great. But they're not what you usually wear to work. Shouldn't you be dressed like you're going to work?"

"Well, yeah, probably, but...I've been thinking and I'm not sure—"

"No. You're not going to get cold feet like Amanda." Chrissy stepped past her, into the entranceway of Josh's townhouse. She paused, looking around, then walked into the living room. Shelby exchanged a worried glance with Amanda before they followed her.

Chrissy grabbed Shelby's bag from the side table and held it out to her. "We're doing this. It's a good plan. Nothing will go wrong."

Shelby took a step back, refusing to take the bag from Chrissy, as if doing so would be like crossing some line with no way back. She glanced over at Amanda and saw the same worried look on her face.

"There's only a million things that *could* go wrong, and just one that could go right. Chrissy, I still think this is a bad idea."

"No, it's not. You have to think positive. If you think everything will go wrong, then it will. But that's not going to happen, because this will work." Chrissy looped the bag over her arm then rummaged through her own, pulling out a tiny recorder. She held it up for both of them to see, a grin on her face. "This is going to be so easy. All you have to do is keep this in your bag and make sure you turn it on, then get David to talk. It shouldn't be that hard."

Shelby shook her head, amused at Chrissy's enthusiasm even as her own sense of impending doom increased. She had thought about this all day yesterday and into the evening, to the point that she had worn herself out with worry until falling asleep on the sofa.

And then Josh had come home and she didn't think to worry anymore. Not about this. No, her worries now were more basic. She had fallen in love with Josh. Maybe she had realized it for some time, deep down inside where she hid things. But last night, she let herself admit the truth.

At least to herself.

Which made Chrissy's idea even more worrisome. It felt too much like lying, even if it was only by omission. What she should do, she realized, is call Josh and tell him she had been fired. Then tell him her suspicions.

That's what she *should* do. She really, really should do just that, knew it without an ounce of doubt. But Chrissy was already dragging both her and Amanda out of the house, slamming the door shut behind her as she herded them down the steps to her car.

And she knew that she was going to get swept up in Chrissy's enthusiasm, that she wasn't going to listen to her instincts or insist that they stop. Because even as she opened her mouth to disagree, Chrissy was herding them both into the car, talking non-stop about what a great plan this was and how nothing could go wrong.

Shelby glanced over at Amanda and noted the expression on her face, realizing it must mirror her own exactly: apprehension coupled with surrender. The two exchanged a glance, then Amanda shook her head.

"We are going to get into so much trouble."

Shelby couldn't help but think the same thing.

**

"Sergeant, there's a Special Agent Levins here to see you."

Josh bit back the oath of impatience that had been ready to tumble from his mouth when he heard the knock on his door frame. Instead he allowed himself a small grumble of frustration and nodded at the cadet, motioning for him to show the visitor in. The kid moved his head in a vague motion of understanding then scrambled back into the hallway, not hiding his eagerness to escape. Josh almost smiled. As easily intimidated as he seemed to be, it would be a small miracle if the kid actually completed all the training necessary to graduate the academy before becoming a police officer.

Or maybe he was just that way with Josh.

Special Agent Levins appeared in the doorway and Josh waved him in, standing briefly to shake the man's hand across the cluttered desk before motioning to the second chair in the small office. From the look on the agent's face, Josh didn't think he had stopped in to announce he had solved the mystery of the who-and-why behind the stolen lock of hair.

"No late-breaking updates, I take it?"

"No, unfortunately." The older man shifted in the creaking chair, taking time to adjust the crease in his dark pants. "I just wanted to come by and thank you for your assistance. As of right now, it looks like we're officially done here. The artifacts are now back in the possession of the Department of the Interior, and they're being moved back to Washington DC for storage. And as much as I'd love to know exactly what happened, it looks like this one may remain a mystery."

Josh nodded, wishing he could say more as the disappointment of untied loose ends spread through him. Despite his casual surface acceptance last night when he explained it to Shelby, he didn't like having unsolved cases. And he didn't like knowing that someone was getting away with something. Granted, this wasn't his case, not really. He merely acted as a liaison. That didn't ease the sting of knowing someone was getting away with something.

"I really wish there was something else I could help with. I don't like leaving loose ends."

"I agree. But at least the items are now back in federal custody. I am sorry to hear about your friend, though. That shouldn't have happened."

Josh stared at the agent for a second, wondering who he was referring to. Then he realized he must mean Shelby, and was beginning to shrug off the agent's concern, surprised that he had heard about her empty arrest. But Levins was already standing, still talking.

"Personally, there was no need for her to be fired. But I guess the museum thought differently. Now that the exhibit is being cancelled—"

"Wait. Wait a minute. Back up. What did you just say?"

"The exhibit is cancelled?"

"No. The other. Shelby got fired?"

Levins paused half-way to the door then reversed direction, all of two feet, and sat back down, giving Josh a disbelieving look. And was it any wonder? His girlfriend gets fired and he doesn't even know it? What kind of cop did that make him?

"Yes, apparently. I spoke with Dr. Spear yesterday evening, and he told me that the museum decided to release Dr. Martin from her contract based on the incident the other day. Like I said, personally I think it was overkill. I also think Dr. Spear was more pleased with the decision to terminate her than he was upset about the exhibit being cancelled."

Josh leaned back in his chair, ignoring the protesting squeal as he studied Levins. Anger mixed with suspicion, making his internal instincts shriek an alarm. "When did they fire her?"

"From what I understand, he called her and left a message the other day."

"A message?" Some of Josh's anger subsided. Shelby may not have even received the message. But no, that didn't make sense. She was supposed to go into work today, had even made the comment this morning that it might be a long day because she would have so much more to do to get caught up in time for the exhibit opening. She may not have known then she had been fired, but she would have certainly found out by now.

And she would have called. Of that, Josh was certain. Or almost certain.

He leaned forward and yanked the phone off the hook, rapidly punching in the numbers to his house. There was a small pause, then ringing on the other end. He listened, counting until the machine picked up. He disconnected the call then punched in the number to her cell phone. Again he listened, counting the rings until the call went to voice mail. Josh forced back his anger as he listened to the professional lilt of her voice instructing the caller to please leave a message before the tone beeped.

"Yeah, it's me. Call me." He slammed the phone into the cradle then leaned back in his chair, noticing the questioning look from Special Agent Levins.

"Is something wrong?"

"Shelby didn't tell me she got fired. And she was supposed to go back to work today."

"Maybe she never got the message."

"Maybe." Josh closed his eyes and let out a deep breath, pinching the bridge of his nose to head off the suddenly-threatening headache. The more insistent the pounding in his head, the more the pieces seemed to fall in place. No, he corrected. It was the pieces falling into place that were causing the pounding in his head.

"Fuck." He let out another deep breath. "Shelby was due to get a promotion once the exhibit opened. The promotion would have actually put her in a bit higher position than Dr. Spear, one where she wouldn't have to answer to him."

Josh opened his eyes and noticed that the mild curiosity on Special Agent Levins' face had turned into a sharper interest. "Is that a fact?"

"Yeah. And there's more. Apparently Shelby used to be in a relationship with Dr. Spear."

"That's something that would have been nice to know at the beginning." He pulled a small notebook from his inside jacket pocket and flipped through the pages. "One would think that at least one of them would have mentioned it."

Josh didn't think it served any purpose at this point to mention that he didn't think either one would have mentioned it unless asked point-blank. It would have been one of the first questions he would have asked if he had been in charge of the investigation, especially considering how adamant Dr. Spear had been that Shelby was somehow involved in the theft.

"And...Shelby's told me before that she didn't trust Spear. In fact, she told me she wouldn't be surprised he had something to do with it." Josh remembered her trying to tell him more that night in Canton, but he hadn't really paid much attention then, thinking her suspicions were based more on David's comments than anything else. And then he had made sure that Shelby was so distracted from everything that had happened that the subject hadn't come up again.

Until last night, when he mentioned that the case was probably going to be over. With the artifacts recovered and no leads, there was nothing they could do. With no suspects and no confession and no proof, there was nothing they could do.

And Shelby had been upset. Reasonably upset, he thought, given how she had been involved. How she had actually been accused of stealing them.

But upset enough to—?

"Fuck. Dammit. Shit. Fuck." Josh let out another deep breath and pinched the bridge of his nose again, knowing it wouldn't help.

"Is something wrong, Sergeant?"

"I hope not, but with the way things are going, I wouldn't bet on it." Josh pushed his chair back and stood, grabbing his jacket off the back and shrugging it on. He glanced at Special Agent Levins and offered him a tight grimace that he tried to pass off as a smile. "Would you care to go with me?"

Levins stood in one fluid movement and followed Josh out of his office. "Where are we going?"

"To solve the mystery and catch a thief. At the museum. Where I have a feeling we'll also find Shelby trying her hand at police work."

"I beg your pardon? Are you saying she's deliberately putting herself in danger?"

Josh clenched his jaw as he led the way through the hallway and outside. "Only when I catch up with her."

Chapter Twenty-One

Shelby walked down the hallway, trying to look as if she belonged there. The chunky heels of her boots alternately thumped and squeaked with each step she took and she tried not to grimace at the noise. The boots definitely helped her attitude, but they weren't exactly quiet.

"Did you really have to wear those things? People can hear you a mile away." Amanda's voice was a soft hiss, and still it seemed to echo in the quiet. Shelby gave her an impatient look, trying to tell her to keep her voice down. Chrissy interrupted her with a harsh laugh.

"Stop it, you two. You're acting like we're trying to sneak in. We're not sneaking. We belong here, remember?"

"No, Chrissy, we don't. Shelby maybe, but not us."

"No, not even me. I'm the one who got fired, remember?" Shelby exchanged a glum expression with her two friends, then shook her head. "This is stupid. I don't care if anyone sees us or not. Even if I was fired, I still have a right to get my things. C'mon, let's just do this and get it done and over with."

She marched further down the hall, no longer caring about being quiet, no longer caring if anyone saw her. So what if they did? She *did* have a right to get her personal things. Besides, she could always play dumb like Chrissy suggested and pretend she didn't know anything. After all, nobody had personally told her she was fired.

No, of course they didn't. Why would they, when it was easier to just leave a message?

Shelby tried to tamp down the anger that had been growing all morning, knowing it wouldn't do any good. The more she thought about it, though, the angrier she became. It wasn't just about getting fired, or even how she had found out about being fired—though either one was bad enough. She had been up for that promotion. She had worked her butt off for that promotion, putting in countless thankless hours, making sure everything was perfect, going above and beyond just to prove herself.

And that was the worst part, because she shouldn't have *had* to prove herself. No—her personnel file was thick with awards and certificates and letters of recommendation and letters of commendations and letters of recognition and achievement that did more than prove herself. She had so many different letters and certificates she could wallpaper her entire apartment with them and still have plenty left over.

But none of that mattered, all because of that spineless, slimy, worthless David. One callous phrase from him in front of the Board of Directors, questioning her stability, had been enough to cast just the tiniest doubt over her and ruin everything she had already achieved. And in this world, that was more than enough to build a roadblock.

But more than a year had passed since that fateful day when he so callously ruined what she had worked for, and Shelby had been sure—positive—that she had moved past that, that she had proved David's careless remark had stemmed from his own personal spite. The promotion had been hers. She had even received assurances from several of the board members about it. As soon as the exhibit opened, the promotion would have been hers. The promotion, and a position just a little bit higher than David. A position that would have required David answer to *her* in some things.

It was supposed to be her quiet justice.

But now, all of that was gone.

Because of David.

Again.

And Shelby knew, without a doubt, that he had been behind the whole thing. She just knew it.

Now all she had to do was prove it.

They had finally reached her office. Shelby reached for the doorknob and turned it, hard enough that she thought it should pop off in her hand. But of course it didn't. It was locked.

She jammed the key into the lock, only a little surprised that it still worked, that the lock hadn't been changed. She pulled the key out and pushed open the door, not caring that she pushed it so hard that it banged against the inside wall and bounced back, nearly hitting her when she stepped into the room. She reached out with her right hand to steady the door while her left hand flipped the light switch and bathed the room in harsh white light.

Shelby sucked her breath in so fast she almost coughed. The sound was echoed behind her by Chrissy and Amanda both as the three of them stared in shock.

Seeing the space empty of her desk and cabinets and shelving was shocking enough. But it was the trash thrown on the floor, the destruction that had been left behind, that seared Shelby from the inside out. Her hands balled into fists by her sides as her gaze swept the space that had once been hers.

Glancing around, she could tell that most everything had been removed. But what remained—her personal things—had been destroyed. And there was no doubt that the destruction had been malicious and deliberate.

She took a hesitant step into the room and felt something crack and crunch under her foot. She looked down and bit back her cry of dismay at the shattered glass and mangled frame that had once housed her diploma.

Shelby stared down at it, her dismay fermenting, changing, morphing into something dark and dangerous. She kicked the mangled fragments away from her with a small cry of fury and looked around at the remaining devastation.

Framed pictures that had once adorned the office walls were now tattered shreds mangled amidst shattered glass. Remnants of small knick-knacks were nothing more than shards littering the tile floor. Not everything of hers had been destroyed, she could see that despite the carnage in front of her. But enough had been.

More than enough.

Shelby blinked and looked around the room again, surprised by the red haze that blurred the edges of her vision. She swallowed, trying to get rid of the burn that was building deep inside her as her fists balled tighter, her nails digging painfully into her palms.

The burn continued, deep-seated, building, becoming an inferno that threatened to consume her until she disappeared into a pile of ash. Her anger simmered, built, and finally boiled over.

"Dammit! Damn him! Damn him!" Shelby stormed into the room, not worrying about the crunching under feet. She kicked at a twisted frame and sent it flying, then stared down at what used to be her Felix the Cat clock. It had been a whimsical thing, nothing more than black plastic and oversized googly eyes and a silly tail that swung back and forth with the passing of each second. Now it was smashed into dozens of pieces. Shelby kicked the mangled plastic into the wall with a shriek. "Damn him!"

"Shelby, stop. C'mon, we should leave."

She shrugged Amanda's hand from her arm and shook her head, her eyes still taking in the destruction surrounding her, understanding but not really comprehending. Her gaze caught on a piece of brown fluff in the corner, partially covered by poor Felix's mangled and decapitated head. She swallowed and walked closer, bending down to pick up the fluff.

Her heart constricted when she recognized it. Or rather, recognized what it used to be. The fluff used to be the floppy arm of the silly Sock Monkey Josh had given her in Annapolis. And the last time she had seen Sock Monkey had been in her apartment the Monday morning she had been arrested. She had looked for him yesterday when she went to pick up some of her things, but didn't really question it when she couldn't find him, thinking maybe she had left him on the boat or in Josh's car.

Now, the sight of the disemboweled and

quartered stuffed animal broke her. Shelby straightened with a growl, the Sock Monkey's amputated arm clutched in her fist. The bastard had been inside her apartment. He broke into her apartment and stole her things. He mutilated Mr. Sock Monkey. Decapitating Felix the Cat was bad enough, but the bastard had mutilated Mr. Sock Monkey!

Shelby stormed across the room, pushing past both Chrissy and Amanda as they tried to grab her.

"Shelby, stop."

"What are you doing?"

"I'm going after him. The bastard had no right to do this. None. And now I'm going after him."

Still clutching Mr. Sock Monkey's amputated arm in her hand, she reached into her bag and fumbled for the tape recorder, pressing the record button by touch. Then she stormed out of the destruction that used to be her work space and headed for David's office, not caring that Chrissy and Amanda had to hurry to keep up with her, not caring that she was now drawing the attention of the few people she passed. By the time she was finished, she would have the attention of everyone in the building.

And she would have David's confession.

Even if she had to rip off his arms like he had ripped off Mr. Sock Monkey's arms.

Chapter Twenty-Two

Josh knew there was trouble as soon as he opened the large double doors to the museum. He didn't need any kind of instinct to tell him, either. No, the crowd of people gathered in the entranceway and milling along the hallway was a good sign that something wasn't right.

If that wasn't enough of an indication, the distant yelling that echoed from deep inside the marbled walls was. The sound was too indistinct to make out words but he had no problem identifying the tone.

Someone was pissed. Seriously pissed.

And a second someone was cajoling and defensive.

Josh had no problem identifying the first someone. Even standing inside the lobby area, he could make out Shelby's voice. Even from this distance, he could tell she was not happy.

Which was probably an understatement, considering the tone and volume echoing back at the crowd.

He cast a quick glance around the crowd, watching their faces, studying their body language. Most were curious, some even looked amused or satisfied. None of them looked concerned or inclined to get closer.

Josh shook his head and grunted at just one more example of the differences in Shelby's world. If such an obvious confrontation had been taking place anywhere else, he'd have to climb over a rowdy crowd just to get close, and probably have to knock some heads together while he was at it. But not here. No, despite the curiosity, there was still a sense of quiet reservation and detachment in the crowd.

It was slightly less than a miracle that the life hadn't been sucked out of Shelby while she worked here.

"Hunh."

"Sergeant?"

Josh turned toward Agent Levins then shook his head, not bothering to explain his audible grunt. "Nothing, just thinking out loud."

The shouting grew louder and Josh actually winced. Levins looked over at him again, no doubt wondering why they weren't moving toward the commotion. Josh sighed, not wanting to ruin Shelby's chance at payback.

Because there was no doubt in his mind who the other person was. If it was up to him, he'd turn around and go back outside for at least a little while longer, just to give Shelby a chance to really let that pompous ass have it. But Levins was giving him a strange look and a few people were beginning to take notice of the two of them standing there, doing nothing. Josh figured it would look really strange if he decided to just turn around and walk out. No matter how tempting it was, he couldn't.

He really couldn't.

Josh took a deep breath and let it out in a heavy sigh, then nodded at Agent Levins before moving into the crowd. They let them through with no problems, parting in front of them with barely-curious glances. Yet another indication of how different his world was from Shelby's.

The respectful calmness of the crowd was only mildly deceptive. They were calm, yes, but by no means completely quiet. Josh heard snippets of conversation and muttered comments as they moved through the crowd.

"...can't believe she was fired..."

"...hope he gets what's coming to him..."

"...don't understand why he's still working here..."

"...about time someone shows him..."

"...that's what she gets for sleeping with him in the first place..."

That final comment caused Josh to pause. But when he would have searched the crowd for the speaker, when he would have stopped and done much more than give the speaker a piece of his mind, a hand closed on his shoulder and nudged him forward. He didn't have to look to know it was Agent Levins.

"Not now, Sergeant." The agent's voice was pitched low, audible only to Josh. He nodded to indicate he had heard and continued pushing his way forward.

The crowd finally thinned as they turned into a hallway. All the doors were closed except for the second one on the right, which was open just enough for everyone to see the indignant woman confronting the frazzled man standing less than a foot away from her. Josh stopped, his gaze momentarily resting on the sight of Shelby standing there. Her back was to him, but he could see she stood tall and confident, not backing down as she waved something in the doctor's face.

Josh squinted at the object in her hand, thinking it looked vaguely familiar but not being able to place it. Movement from the corner of his eye caught his attention and he turned his head, narrowing his gaze on the two women who were trying to melt into the crowd behind them.

"You two. Freeze. Now."

The two women looked like they wanted to turn and run, but they froze in place. The taller of the two lifted her chin higher, defiance sparkling in her clear eyes. Chrissy, he thought her name was. Josh recognized her as the voluptuous blonde from that night in the bar. He wondered if she had been the one who had urged Shelby on that silly dare to pick him up. If she was, he would have to thank her.

But not right now.

Right now, he had other things he had to do.

The voices in the office were getting louder, if that was even possible. Josh shook his head and let out a heavy sigh, then motioned to Agent Levins. As much as he didn't want to, it was time to put a stop to the show.

"You're a low-life, sneaky, lying bastard, and you know it!"

"Really, Shelby, you're being melodramatic."

"Melodramatic? You're a thief! You stole those artifacts and tried to blame everything on me!"

"I did not 'steal' them. They were completely safe the entire time. How was I to know someone would call the police and FBI and everyone else?"

Josh and Agent Levins both stopped and looked at each as the implication of the doctor's words hit them.

"Oh my God! You admit it then! You stole them, and you broke into my apartment and stole my things, too." Shelby stepped closer and waved something small and furry in the doctor's face. Something white fluttered to the ground and Josh squinted again, trying to focus on the object in Shelby's hand. What the hell? It couldn't be...could it?

"You stole my things, and you mutilated them. You're a thief and a...a...you're a murderer! You're a murdering bastard!"

Josh risked a glance at Agent Levins and noticed that he seemed to be having trouble keeping a straight face. He ran a hand over his own mouth, fighting the urge to laugh, and knew he should do something. Like maybe make his presence known. Something...

"Oh please. I didn't 'break-in'. I used a key. Really, I can't believe you didn't have the locks changed after a year. As to that...that *thing*...so what? It was just some stupid stuffed animal. Absolutely worthless. Completely unimportant."

A shriek ripped the air, a wailing sound that brought to mind banshees and ghosts. Before Josh could react, Shelby lunged toward the doctor, her arms flailing wildly. "You lying bastard! How could you? You're a murderer! A murdering monkey mutilator!"

Josh and Agent Levins moved forward together, entering the room and getting between the two. Josh wrapped his arms around Shelby's waist and spun her around, pulling her away from her frantic attack. Her legs kicked wildly, the heel of one of her boots catching him in the shin. Josh grunted but didn't release her, just made soothing sounds in her ear, trying to calm her down.

"Agent! Thank God you're here! Did you see her attack me? For no reason! I'm pressing charges! I demand you arrest her immediately!" David straightened, his back ramrod straight as he leveled an accusing finger at Shelby.

"Me? You're the one who needs to be arrested!"

Josh tightened his arms around her waist and pulled her closer against him. "Shelby, stop. You need to calm down."

"Calm down? Did you see what he did? Look! Just look!" She struggled in his arms, finally freeing herself and turning toward him, waving the piece of brown fluff in his face. "He killed Mr. Sock Monkey!"

Agent Levins moved toward the doctor, grabbing his arms and turning him so he was pushed against the desk. The click of the handcuffs being closed around his pale wrists echoed the room, followed by his gasp of outrage.

"What are you doing? I demand you release me immediately. You have no right—"

"Dr. David Spear, you're under arrest."

"For what? I've done nothing! You have no proof—"

"Theft of government property, to start." Levins paused and looked over at the brown fluff Shelby continued to wave. His lips briefly twitched and he shook his head. "And destruction of private property."

"You can't do this! You stupid, silly bitch. You won't get away—" The doctor's words were cut-off as Agent Levins jerked on his handcuffs and pushed him from the room, reciting his rights as he led him away.

Josh let out a deep breath, then fixed Shelby with a stern gaze meant to intimidate the harshest of men.

But the gaze was wasted, because Shelby wasn't even looking at him—she was staring after the retreating men, her eyes squinting in an unreadable expression. Before Josh could act, she took off after them, muttering to herself. He had no idea what she had planned on doing, no idea what kind of hare-brained impulse drove her, but he wasn't going to wait to find out. He took two steps and grabbed her around the waist, then turned her around and tossed her over his shoulder. She grunted in surprise, then started kicking with her legs. Josh steadied her with a firm hand on the curve of her bottom, gently pinching.

"Unless you want to be publicly spanked in front of your colleagues, I suggest you stop struggling and go peacefully." His words were pitched low enough that only Shelby could hear, and she stilled immediately. He gave her luscious bottom one more squeeze then started down the hallway, pausing only long enough to give her two friends a stern look. "You two, follow me. Now."

The two women gave each other a worried glance and Josh could clearly see the trepidation in their expressions. But they fell in behind him, muttering comforting words to Shelby as she hung upside down over his shoulder. Josh rolled his eyes and bit back his smile, wondering what the gathered crowd thought of their unusual departure. From the whispered comments, he was certain Shelby had reached martyr status in their eyes.

He shook his head and muttered to himself as he pushed his way out the door to his waiting car, wondering what in the hell he was going to do next.

Chapter Twenty-Three

Shelby wrapped her arms more tightly around her middle and tried to control her breathing. Deep breath in, deep breath out. Another chill went through her, and she gave up on the breathing exercises and instead looked around the room. The walls were a weird gray-green and water stains marred the old ceiling tiles. She briefly wondered if they were asbestos tiles, and if she would have to worry about contracting some kind of respiratory disease in the immediate future.

The table in front of her was nothing more than a beat up rectangular table: four metal legs painted brown with a scarred top that may have resembled a wood grain at some time in the last decade. The only thing it resembled now was a cast-off that belonged in an old abandoned warehouse somewhere. Despite its dilapidation, Shelby was still tempted to rest her head on it and close her eyes, just so she wouldn't have to stare around the room. She would have done just that, except for two things: one of the table legs was shorter than the others, which caused the table to lean and wobble.

And there was some kind of stain on the surface that she really didn't want to examine too closely. In fact, there were several stains she didn't want to examine too closely.

She took in another deep breath and slid her chair a little further away from the table. This could be the same room she had been in before...maybe. Shelby couldn't say for sure.

Just like she couldn't say for sure if she was under arrest.

Josh hadn't said one word to her since carrying her out of the building. He had simply placed her in his car and drove her to the police station, then unceremoniously left her here in this room. The word 'dumped' came to mind, but in all fairness he hadn't physically dumped her anywhere. He simply walked her through the precinct, guiding her past curious stares with a steady hand at her back, then left her here in this room. He had given her an unreadable look and shook his head, then simply walked out.

At least he hadn't carried her in over his shoulder like he had back at the museum. That had been embarrassing enough as it was.

And he hadn't handcuffed her, which Shelby hoped was a good sign.

At least, that's what she told herself. The last time she had been arrested, she had been handcuffed, so maybe that meant she wasn't really arrested.

But if she wasn't under arrest, then why was she here? And where were Amanda and Chrissy? Shelby knew they were somewhere around here, because she had seen them walk in behind her. She just didn't know where they were now. Were they under arrest, too?

The whole situation could have gone so much better, but Shelby knew they had been lucky...because it could have gone so much worse. Although, she thought, being back in this room definitely fell into the category of 'worse'. Protests of unfairness and false arrest came to mind, but Shelby couldn't bring herself to utter them out loud. Not that there was anyone to protest to, since she had been in the room by herself for at least an hour so far. That's what it felt like, anyway.

But in all fairness, she had to admit—at least to herself—that she knew something like this could happen. Her gut had been gnawing at her since yesterday afternoon, and some kind of instinct had been screaming at her since Chrissy and Amanda had picked her up a few hours ago.

Okay, so maybe they should have gone about the whole thing differently. Maybe she should have told Josh what she thought and what they planned to do. But she didn't, and now she would have to pay the price. But at least she had the recording of David confessing. The slimy bastard. She still couldn't believe he had been behind everything! Well, part of her could believe it...but she still didn't understand *why*. Why would he want to frame her like that? Just to get her fired? Was he that petty and vile and malicious?

An image of the mutilated stuffed animal came to mind, answering her own questions. Yes, he really was that petty and vile and malicious.

Well, he would get what he deserved. At least, she hoped he would.

Which still didn't explain why she was sitting here in this room, all by herself.

Shelby pushed away from the table and stood up,

briefly stretching to relieve the tightness in her legs. Her gaze swept around the room once more before finally settling on the hazy mirror in the middle of the far wall. She had seen enough shows to know it was a two-way mirror, not that it took any great intelligence to figure it out. Was Josh behind that mirror now, watching her? Or maybe that other agent was. Or maybe it was someone completely different, a group of people just watching her to see what she would do. That's what they did on television.

She shivered at the creepy thought then walked over to the mirror and tapped on it with her knuckles.

"Hello? If you're there and you're watching me, could you please stop? And is Josh there? Josh, how long do I have to stay here? Am I under arrest again? Can I go home? Is anyone there? Hello? Hello?"

The door opened behind her and she whirled around, startled. Josh stood in the doorway, watching her with his unreadable cop-face. Shelby clasped her hands in front of her, suddenly feeling guilty for no reason at all.

"Who are you talking to?"

"Um..." She shrugged and pointed to the mirror behind her. "The people behind the mirror."

Josh continued to watch her for a long minute then slowly shook his head and crooked one finger in the universal signal to "come here". Shelby thought about ignoring him, then decided that probably wasn't the smartest thing to do.

He held the door open for her then took two steps toward the door next to the room she had just left. He gave her a pointed glance and opened the door, motioning for her to look in. So he was going to let her see who was watching her? Shelby held her breath and peered around the door jamb, wondering who she would see...

And looked straight into the musty interior of a poorly-lit utility closet.

Josh shook his head, closed the closet door, and led her back into the other room.

"I thought it was a two-way mirror," Shelby admitted as Josh closed the door. He gave her another unreadable look then walked across the room and pulled out one of the chairs. He spun it backwards and straddled it, then leaned forward and rested his elbows on the table.

"That's just for show. If we really want to watch you, we use that." He pointed behind her and Shelby turned. Mounted high in the corner, obvious to anyone who cared to look, was a dusty video camera. Shelby glared at it, thinking it completely unfair that she didn't notice it earlier and trying to blame the camera for her own lack of observation skills.

She turned back around and noticed that Josh was still looking at her with that unreadable gaze. Shelby shifted her weight from one foot to the other, at a loss of what she should say or do, if anything. Josh finally nodded but it wasn't at her, it was at the chair across from him.

"Sit down." It wasn't really an order, and there was nothing ominous in his tone, but Shelby couldn't shake the feeling she was in some kind of trouble. She hesitated, probably just a minute too long because Josh took a deep breath and reached up to pinch the bridge of his nose before letting out a heavy sigh. "Shelby, please. Have a seat."

The weariness in his voice surprised her and she hurried over to the chair and slid it out, nearly knocking it over in her haste to sit. She stood up as straight as she could and folded her hands in her lap, still not willing to touch the table and come in contact with whatever criminal crud coated the marred surface. She thought she heard Josh mutter something but she couldn't make out what it was, and his mouth was tightly closed when she finally looked up at him. A small twitch marred his left cheek, just the briefest movement, and she wondered why he was clenching his jaw.

The silence stretched around them for so long that she began to fidget in her chair, wondering if she should say something at the exact same time Josh let out a short laugh.

"I have no idea where to even begin."

Shelby stilled at his words, confusion causing her to open her mouth. No sound came out, which was just as well because Josh shook his head and motioned for her to be quiet. Her jaw snapped shut with an audible click and she lowered her gaze to her tightly clenched hands.

"I don't know whether to laugh, ring your neck, or arrest you."

Shelby swallowed against the thickness in her throat and peered at him through her lashes, afraid to fully look at him. "Um...arrest?"

"Is that a question? Or a suggestion?" She didn't know how to answer that either, so she offered him a half-hearted shrug and went back to studying her hands. She thought she heard him chuckle but she couldn't be sure and she was afraid to look up at him. "As tempting as that may be, there's nothing to arrest you for. Harebrained idiocy isn't a crime."

"Idiocy?" Her voice came out as an undignified

squeak but she didn't care. Her head snapped up and she shot Josh her own impatient glare, which would have been more effective if she hadn't seen the small twitch of his lips. "You're laughing at me!"

Josh brushed his hand across his mouth and shook his head. "No. 'Laughing' isn't quite the word I'd use. I would say 'amused', but that's not even quite right. It's more...well, let's just say I'm trying to find some humor in the situation before I really do ring your neck."

"Why do you want to ring my neck? I didn't do anything wrong! If anything, I solved the crime for you. I even have his confession on tape!"

"Yes. Yes, you do. And about that..." Josh leaned away from the table and folded his arms across the back of the chair before pinning her in place with a steady gaze. "Why didn't you tell me what you were planning on doing?"

"I...um, I..."

"Why didn't you tell me your suspicions?"

"Um, I thought..."

"Why didn't you tell me you were fired?"

Shelby snapped her mouth shut. She didn't know how to answer that one, and she figured it was better to look pathetic than to sound pathetic. And that was exactly how she sounded, stuttering and mumbling incoherent non-answers. She shook her head again and looked away, not able to meet Josh's stern and steady gaze. Quiet minutes went by, minutes that felt like hours.

"Shelby, look at me."

There was something in Josh's voice, more than just a quiet command. Shelby took a deep breath for courage and finally raised her head. She wasn't prepared for the unguarded look in Josh's deep eyes, for the emotion and disappointment swimming in his dark gaze. The breath lodged in her throat and a ball of angst settled in her stomach but she didn't look away. She couldn't look away.

"Why didn't you tell me you were fired?"

It was a simple question, and she should have been able to give him a simple answer. But she didn't have one, and the truth sounded so lame that she was embarrassed to admit it. To him, to herself.

But Josh kept watching her, his gaze steady and unguarded. Shelby finally looked away, shaking her head and shrugging.

"I don't really know. I just...didn't. I couldn't."

"Why?"

"I'm...I'm not sure. I thought...I was embarrassed. I was afraid if I told you, you'd..."

"I'd...what? Think less of you? Go after Spear? All of the above? Something else? What?"

Shelby picked at her thumb nail, afraid to look at him. She swallowed back her nervousness and shrugged again. "A little of all of it, I guess."

"For Chrissakes Shelby..." She heard the frustration in his voice and looked up at him again, surprised to see his face buried in his hands. She wasn't sure what that meant, if he was angry or upset or disappointed. The ball in her stomach turned into a knot, and she took a deep breath to get rid of it.

"Um, what happens now?" Her words were barely above a whisper, and she hated herself for it. Where did all the fire going through her before disappear to? She closed her eyes and willed it to come back, told herself that she was a different person now, that she was strong and feisty. But it didn't work, no matter how many times she repeated it to herself.

Josh finally removed his hands from his face and looked at her, his gaze as tired as his sigh. He shook his head and pushed himself to his feet. "Now? I get to go process the bad guy, and you go home."

"Home?" The knot in Shelby's stomach grew even bigger. He was telling her to go home, just like that? He was ending everything, just like that? Her mind went blank and her body went numb for a terrifying minute. Then she just nodded and stood on shaky legs, the chunky boots on her feet making it feel like she was walking through quick-drying cement that threatened to suck her under. She wished she had some snappy comment for Josh, some eloquent phrase that would make her sound sophisticated and worldly, but her mind came up blank.

She glanced back at him just before she reached the door, thinking she should say something, anything, when his phone rang. He looked down at the screen and muttered under his breath then answered it.

Shelby sighed to herself and turned back for the door, thinking it was probably better if she just left without saying anything. Because if she did, she'd probably make a fool of herself.

"Shelby?"

She paused at Josh's voice, wondering if she should even turn around. She blinked to clear her eyes and told herself she could be mature about this, that there was no reason for silly emotions. She pasted a plastic smile on her face and half-turned toward him.

"Try to stay out of trouble, okay?"

Her mouth dropped open and for a split-second she felt the fire flare to life inside her once more. Stay out of trouble? That's all he had to say? But Josh had focused his attention on the phone call, his face once again schooled into his featureless cop mask. Shelby snapped her mouth closed and yanked the door open so quickly she almost hit herself with it. Her face heated with embarrassment and she was glad he wasn't watching her. The fire flared inside her a bit more as she walked through the door, and she slammed it behind her with as much force as she could muster, taking a perverse satisfaction in the loud noise that echoed along the hallway as she left.

Chapter Twenty-Four

Josh parked the car in front of the house and blew out a long breath. A pounding had started behind his left eye about three hours ago—which was about six hours after his last meal. He wanted nothing more than to get inside, strip out of his clothes, get something to eat...and then fall into bed with Shelby. Not necessarily in that order.

And definitely not to sleep.

He climbed the few steps to the front door and unlocked it then pushed his way inside, haphazardly tossing his keys onto the small entranceway table. He paused just long enough to drop his bag on the floor and kept walking, focused solely on climbing upstairs to Shelby.

She was probably asleep. Lord knows, it had to have been a long day for her. He was used to it, to crazy schedules and crazy people and the ups-and-downs of adrenaline rushes followed by adrenaline crashes. He was used to the darker side of people, to seeing the worst in society. And yet even he had times where it was too much, where it took its toll.

So no, he wouldn't blame Shelby in the least if she was asleep. If he had finished a little sooner, he would be in bed with her right now, his body pressed tightly against hers as he buried himself deep inside...

He shook off the visual and headed for the stairs leading up to his room...and to Shelby's welcoming body. Yes, he had been a little later than he planned, but it was worth it. Josh glanced down at the furry animal in his hands and couldn't help but smile. The trip to Annapolis and back had taken longer than he had planned, but knowing how Shelby would react when he gave her the small gift, knowing the soft smile that would light up her face and glow deep in her eyes...

Yes, the trip had definitely been worth it.

Josh slowed at the top of the stairs then continued toward the bedroom, his steps muffled by the carpet beneath his feet. He didn't want to wake Shelby by clomping into the room—he had a better way to wake her in mind. He glanced down once more at the package in his hand and smiled again.

He would ease himself into bed next to her, sliding over until their bodies barely touched. Then he would let himself watch her, just for a minute, before nuzzling that sensitive spot just below her ear. When she came awake with that little start of sleepy surprise, he would smile down at her and give her the gift. Actually, he would give her two, because he was certain she would want every detail of what happened after she left. And then...then he planned on making love to her the entire night.

Or at least until his body couldn't function any longer.

Yeah, he could definitely get used to coming home

like this. Would it be easy with him working shift work, especially night work? Not easy, no. But not impossible, either. And if he changed some things up, switched things around so he didn't work every night...yeah, he could do it. He had already talked to his lieutenant and discussed his options, and he had plenty open. And if the lieutenant had been surprised, he hid it well.

So maybe Josh had three surprises for Shelby...

He eased open the bedroom door, wincing at the slight creak of the hinges. He'd have to oil them so they wouldn't be so noisy. It would ruin his plans if Shelby woke up before he had the chance to surprise her.

Josh held his breath and glance at the bed, hoping the noise hadn't wakened her. He blinked and looked again, then let out an oath loud enough to wake the dead. No longer caring about the noise, Josh palmed the light switch and flooded the room with bright light before storming over to the bed.

The empty bed.

"Dammit."

He glanced around the room, noticing what the bright light revealed. The few things of Shelby's that had been here were gone: a few books that had been on the nightstand, a pair of ridiculously fuzzy slippers that had been tucked under her side of the bed, a silly cartoon wind-up alarm clock that she insisted on using because she had a fear of sleeping through a radio alarm.

Gone. Just like Shelby.

"Dammit."

Josh crossed to the bathroom, knowing even before he turned on the light that it, too, would be vacant of any of her things. It didn't take a detective to figure out the obvious: Shelby had packed up and left.

But why?

Josh leaned his shoulder against the doorframe and stared down at the sock monkey in his hand, as if waiting for insight from the piece of fluff. What had he missed? He thought back over the day, replaying every word he and Shelby had exchanged.

Go home.

Was that really it? It couldn't be...

Josh glanced around the two rooms, devoid of Shelby's belongings, devoid of the unique spark that surrounded her. Whether it could be or not was a moot point, because Shelby was gone.

"Dammit."

Josh looked down once more at the fluff in his hand and swore again, then headed out of the room and down the stairs, stopping long enough to grab his keys from where he had tossed them only a few short minutes ago.

**

The sound of the doorbell rang through the apartment, the shrillness breaking the silence. The insistent buzzing would have wakened Shelby from a comatose sleep.

If she had been sleeping.

She muttered under her breath and rolled over, pulling the pillow firmly over her head and willing the noise to stop.

It didn't. Instead, it became steadier, a non-stop nuisance like someone was leaning on the door buzzer.

Bzzzzzzzzzzz.

Bzzzzzzzzzzz.

A pause in the irritating noise filled the space with a deafening silence. Shelby held her breath, torn between giving thanks and rushing out to the door to see if he was still there.

Because there was no doubt who was standing in the hallway outside her apartment with his finger pressed firmly against the doorbell.

Josh.

Shelby flung the pillow to the floor and strained her ears in the silence. She was an idiot. A complete idiot. An over-reacting fool.

And she was too embarrassed to face him.

Shelby rolled over onto her back and stared through the semi-darkness at the ceiling. Part of her wanted to jump from the bed and run after Josh, to apologize for acting like a fool.

Another part of her said she'd only embarrass herself more by running after him, that it would be better to wait and deal with everything in the morning.

But morning could be too late. What if Josh decided it wasn't worth it? Even now he could be getting in his car and driving away.

Her stomach did a sickening roll at the thought and she clenched the edge of the comforter in her fist, frozen with indecision.

Bzzzzzzzzz.

Bzzzzzzzzz.

Bang. Bang. Bang.

Pause.

Bang. Bang. Bang.

The pounding noise provided the impetus for Shelby to move. It was one thing for her to sulk in silence while the buzzer echoed around her; it was something else entirely for her neighbors to be awakened by the loud banging against her door.

She flung the comforter to the side and pushed herself out of bed, her feet silent against the floor as she stumbled out of the room. Her toe caught against the doorframe and she winced as pain shot up her leg.

"Dammit!" Shelby reached down and grabbed her foot, trying to rub her sore toe as she hopped along the hallway.

Bzzzz.

Bang. Bang. Bang.

Bang. Bang. Bang.

"I hear you! Stop! I'm coming!" Shelby limped toward the door and stumbled again, this time banging her shoulder against the wall. "Ouch, dammit!"

Bang. Bang. Bang.

Bang. Bang. Bang.

"I said stop!" Shelby turned the deadbolt and yanked open the door, then had to fight the urge to slam it in Josh's face.

His very serious, very irritated face. Shelby swallowed against her momentary panic then straightened, hoping she looked just as irritated as he did. Josh lifted one brow at her in an expression of mild amusement before resuming a stance more fitting to some old stone statue.

"What are you doing here?"

Shelby had been ready to ask him the same question. She snapped her mouth closed and narrowed her eyes, willing her slow mind to come up with some snappy reply.

"I live here."

Another spark of amusement flashed across his chiselled face, and Shelby had to force herself not to groan out loud at the absurdity of her statement. *I live here*. What a profound and snappy comeback. She angled herself more closely against the door and narrowed her eyes at him again, hoping she looked irritated and put-out.

"What do you want?"

"Are you going to let me in?"

"No. I'm mad at you."

The humor vanished from his face, replaced quickly by a look of astonishment. "Mad at me? What did I do?"

"You told me to go home."

Another expression crossed Josh's face, one she couldn't quite identify. Shelby told herself not to look too closely, though, because she could almost swear it looked like impatience. Her suspicions were reinforced when Josh raised his eyes to the ceiling and mumbled something under his breath before looking back at her.

"You're pouting."

"What? I most certainly am not!" But maybe she was, just a little. Not that it should matter, even if she was. Which she wasn't, not really.

Her heart stammered when he looked back at her with something resembling a twinkle in his dark eyes, and she tightened her grip on the edge of the door in an attempt to force herself not to step closer to him.

Which was really absurd, even in her current state of embarrassment. Why shouldn't she step closer to him? Why shouldn't she just throw herself at him? If she hadn't been so stupid, if she hadn't overreacted earlier, they'd probably be in bed right now.

A rush of warmth flooded her at the thought of exactly what they'd probably be doing in that bed right now. She adjusted her grip on the door, her palms suddenly sweaty. Heat flashed in Josh's eyes as his gaze swept over her.

No, not swept. That implied an action that was entirely too fast for what he was doing. He let his look linger over every inch of her body, made her skin flame beneath the thin shirt and sleeping boxers she wore. His gaze finally rested on her face, heat evident in his eyes. The corner of his mouth edged up in a slight smile that was just as dangerous to her sanity.

"Let me in, Shelby." The heat in his eyes was nothing compared to the warmth of his voice, low and husky and promising. She swallowed, suddenly nervous.

No, not nervous. Her nerves were definitely humming, but this had nothing to do with being nervous. Anxious, yes. But in a way that had her struggling to remember why she shouldn't be yanking him through the open door instead of making him stand there in the hallway.

"I have something for you." Promise glinted in his eyes, heating her even further, and she tried to think of something sassy and witty to say. She opened her mouth, hoping the witty words would tumble from her lips without too much thought on her part.

But instead of something sophisticatedly sassy, a squeal of surprise left her in a rush. Josh had pulled something from behind his back and held it out to her with a boyish flourish that was so at odds with what she knew of him that she actually took a surprised step backwards.

Right into the edge of the door.

Ignoring his muffled laughter, she pushed the door open further, out of her way, and reached out for the stuffed little animal.

"Mr. Sock Monkey! You got me a new one!" The

tips of her fingers brushed the monkey's arms but Josh pulled it away before she could take it, holding it above his head, out of her reach.

"Nope, not unless you let me in."

Shelby stepped back without thought, opening the door wider and motioning for him to come in. Josh laughed and stepped past her, finally holding the stuffed monkey out for her once she closed the door. She looked down at it, dangling from his hand like an offering of gold.

An image of her other sock monkey, the one Josh had bought her on their trip to Annapolis, flashed through her mind. She bit her lip, remembering how the poor little thing had been butchered and mutilated out of spite. She reached out and took the new one in her hand, cuddling it in her palm before tucking it under her chin.

This new monkey was exactly like the old one, down to the Navy football jersey it wore. Shelby blinked against the moisture building behind her lids and offered Josh a bright smile. "Where did you get him?"

"Um," Josh looked away and cleared his throat, then looked back at her with an almost embarrassed shrug. "I drove down to Annapolis to get him for you tonight."

"Oh, Josh! Thank you!" Shelby couldn't hold back any longer. She closed the short distance between them and jumped into his arms. Josh stumbled then steadied himself, closing his arms around her as she wrapped her legs around his waist.

"Thank you! I can't believe you drove all the way down there tonight to get him. You have no idea how much this means!" She leaned forward and pressed her lips against his in a quick kiss then leaned back and smiled at him.

"Hmm. I think I do." He pulled her tighter against him, adjusting his hold as he moved through the living room. "You would have had him sooner, if you hadn't disappeared."

"I didn't disappear. You told me to go home."

"You know what I meant."

She buried her face in his shoulder and shrugged, tightening her arms around him. "I thought I knew what you meant, but I was upset and I wasn't sure. I thought you were mad at me and..."

"I was mad at you. And mad at myself. And mad at that idiot." Josh paused at the entrance of the bedroom door, his gaze growing serious as he looked down at her. "You could have been hurt, and it would have been my fault. I should have known something wasn't right."

Shelby placed the tips of her fingers against his mouth, quieting him. "Shh. It doesn't matter. It's over now." She frowned and shot him a questioning look. "It is over, right?"

"The bad guy got his." A shiver swept through her when he drew the tip of her finger into his mouth and nipped it lightly. "And...you have your job back."

Shelby's breath hitched in her chest but it had nothing to do with Josh's words...and everything to do with the gentle pressure of him sucking her finger. "I...I do?"

"Mmm hmm."

Josh moved more slowly now, closer to the bed. She could feel the motion of his body against hers, feel the move and play of hard muscles as he laid her back against the bed and came down on top of her. His mouth found hers, gentle in his claiming, hot in his possessiveness until he broke away with a groan and looked down at her.

Even in the soft darkness she could see the heat in his gaze, feel it stroke her skin, calling the heat inside her, demanding an answer. His hands slipped under her shirt and eased it up, the tips of his fingers scraping the underside of her aching breasts. He lowered his head and took a taut nipple into his mouth, sucking and laving until she wrapped her legs tighter around his waist and arched up, rubbing against the hard length of his erection.

Josh shifted his weight, moving his arms to either side of her head and capturing her face in his hands. "And...you have me. If you want me."

"Oh Josh." Shelby blinked against the emotion so clear in his dark eyes and nodded. "Yes. Yes, I want you."

Josh claimed her mouth in a searing kiss, barely pulling away so she could catch her breath. "I love you, Shelby."

Her breath hitched and for a long moment she couldn't breathe, couldn't think against the swimming in her mind, couldn't hear past the thundering beat of her heart. Everything tilted around her for one terrifying minute, leaving her dizzy and afraid.

And then the world straightened with a defining *click* and for the first time, everything around her shone bright and clear. "Oh Josh. I love you too!"

She tugged the sock monkey from between them and tossed it to the floor, giving Josh an apologetic shrug at his questioning glance. "We can't corrupt the poor guy."

Josh laughed, then claimed her mouth in another

searing kiss. Their clothes disappeared with little effort, falling into a discarded pile on the floor.

Shelby arched against him, searching, crying out when Josh entered her in a hard thrust she felt to the very edge of her soul.

And she knew, without a doubt, that the dangerous passion that flared between them was the safest place for her to be.

*****

DANGEROUS PASSION

Lisa B. Kamps

ABOUT THE AUTHOR

Lisa B. Kamps is the author of the best-selling series *The Baltimore Banners*, featuring "hard-hitting, heart-melting hockey players" (USA Today), on and off the ice. Her newest series, *Firehouse Fourteen*, features hot and heroic firefighters who put more than their lives on the line.

In a previous life, she worked as a firefighter with the Baltimore County Fire Department, then did a very brief (and not very successful) stint at bartending in east Baltimore, and finally served as the Director of Retail Operations for a busy Civil War non-profit.

Lisa currently lives in Maryland with her husband and two sons (who are mostly sorta-kinda out of the house), one very spoiled Border Collie, two cats with major attitude, several head of cattle, and entirely too many chickens to count. When she's not busy writing or chasing animals, she's cheering loudly for her favorite hockey team, the Washington Capitals--or going through withdrawal and waiting for October to roll back around!

Interested in reaching out to Lisa? She'd love to hear from you, and there are several ways to contact her:

Website: www.LisaBKamps.com
Newsletter: www.lisabkamps.com/signup/
Email: LisaBKamps@gmail.com
Facebook Author Page:
www.facebook.com/authorLisaBKamps
Kamps Korner Facebook Group:
www.facebook.com/groups/1160217000707067/
Twitter: twitter.com/LBKamps

Goodreads: www.goodreads.com/LBKamps
Amazon Author Page:
www.amazon.com/author/lisabkamps
Instagram: www.instagram.com/lbkamps/
BookBub: www.bookbub.com/authors/lisa-b-kamps

ONCE BURNED
Firehouse Fourteen Book 1

Michaela Donaldson had her whole life planned out: college, music, and a happy-ever-after with her first true love. One reckless night changed all that, setting Michaela on a new path. Gone are her dreams of pursuing music in college, replaced by what she thinks is a more rewarding life. She's a firefighter now, getting down and dirty while doing her job. So what if she's a little rough around the edges, a little too careless, a little too detached? She's happy, living life on her own terms--until Nicky Lansing shows back up.

Nick Lansing was the stereotypical leather-clad bad boy, needing nothing but his fast car, his guitar, his never-ending partying, and his long-time girlfriend-- until one bad decision changed the course of two lives forever. He's on the straight-and-narrow now, living life as a respected teacher and doing his best to be a positive role model. Yes, he still has his music. But gone are his days of partying. And gone is the one girl who always held his heart. Or is she?

One freak accident brings these two opposites back together. Is ten years long enough to heal the physical and emotional wounds from the past? Can they reconcile who they were with who they've become--or will it be a case of Once Burned is enough?

***Turn the page for an exciting peek at* ONCE BURNED,** *available now.*

"Oh shit," Mike repeated under her breath, too horrified to do anything more than force herself to breathe. Not an easy task, considering she was literally frozen to the spot. The air was thick with heated tension and the buzzing in her ears made it impossible for her to hear anything. She willed herself to move, to do something.

Shit, it's Nicky. Shit, it's Nicky. The phrase kept spinning through her mind until she thought she'd be sick with the dizziness of it. Her chest heaved with the effort to breathe and her pulse beat in a tap dancer's rhythm.

Did anyone else notice the sudden change in the room? Mike forced herself to look away from that face from her past and quickly glanced around. Four sets of eyes fixed on her with varying degrees of bewilderment. She could still feel *his* eyes on her, too, filled with stunned disbelief.

Feeling like she was trapped in a nightmare where everything moved with the speed of molasses, Mike pushed away from the counter and walked across the room, straight past the frozen figure of Nicky Lansing and through the swinging door. She turned a corner and rushed through a second door that opened into the engine room, not stopping until she reached the engine on the far side, where she promptly collapsed on the back step.

Heedless of the dirt and grime, she let her head drop against the back compartment door, ignoring the length of hose line in her way. Her breathing came in shallow gasps that did nothing to help the lightheadedness that caused black dots to dance across her closed lids.

Hyperventilating. She was hyperventilating. The

calm, rational part of her—she was surprised she still had one—told her to lean forward, to get a grip on herself and her breathing. Now bent over, sitting with her head between her knees, Mike grabbed the running board with both hands and concentrated on the feel of the diamond plate cutting into her palms.

The spots faded away and her breathing slowed to something closer to normal. One last deep breath and she straightened, only to choke on a scream when she came face-to-face with Jay, his brows lowered in a frown as he studied her with concern.

"Jesus! Don't scare me like that!" She pushed him away then stood, only to sit back down when she realized how bad her knees were shaking.

"Scare *you*? What is wrong with you? Are you okay?"

"I'm fine. I couldn't be better! Don't I look fine?"

"You look like you're ready to pass out. What the hell is going on? Do you know that guy? He looks like he's seen a ghost!"

"He probably thinks he has." Mike moved over and motioned for Jay to sit down, ignoring his scrutiny as he twisted sideways and continued staring at her.

"Are you going to explain that?"

"No." She ran her hands through her hair, muttering when she pulled a thick hank of it loose from the pony tail. Sighing, she reached back and pulled the elastic band loose, then quickly rearranged her hair into a more secure hold. Jay watched her intently then nudged her leg with his when she continued to ignore him.

"Well?"

"Well nothing. He's just somebody I used to know, that's all."

Jay snorted. "Bull."

"Okay, fine," she conceded grudgingly. "He's also somebody I never wanted to see again." Mike reached down and gingerly touched her right side, trying not to remember but unable to forget. If Jay noticed the motion, he didn't say anything.

They sat in silence, the familiar background noises of the station virtually unnoticed. A few minutes went by before Jay spoke again. "You sure you don't want to talk about it?"

Mike shook her head, ready to make a sarcastic reply when the sound of footsteps echoed through the engine room. The steps paused, then changed directions and hesitantly walked around the side of the engine. Mike knew without looking who it was: the steps were those of a stranger, someone who didn't know his way around.

Nicky stopped at the back of the engine, not saying anything as Jay slowly stood and positioned himself slightly in front of Mike, shielding her. She touched his arm briefly, in a gesture both of thanks and of reassurance that she was alright. Jay looked back at her, one brow cocked in question, then reluctantly walked away at her nod. Mike didn't see where he went but knew that he would be close by in case he was needed.

She stood slightly, leaning against the running board, then crossed her arms in front of her, covering the jagged scar that ran along her left forearm. The stance was as close to aloof and detached as she could manage considering her insides were making a milkshake of her early dinner. Too late, she remembered the sunglasses hanging around her neck and wished she would have thought to put them on to hide any emotion in her eyes.

With an effort that took more strength than she wanted to admit, she let her eyes slowly, coolly rake the man in front of her from top to bottom.

Dammit. The Nicky Lansing from her past had been ruggedly handsome with dark looks and boyish charm; this Nick Lansing was dangerously gorgeous. A little taller than she remembered, he stood just over six feet, and was definitely broader through the shoulders and chest. The boy she remembered had finally filled out, to all the best advantages.

The long hair of his past was gone, cut to a length that brushed just past the collar of the light blue shirt he wore. Still too long to be squeaky clean, but short enough by today's standards to be rated as acceptable. His eyes were the same, though. A dark chocolate brown framed in long lashes, they invited a person to swim in their depths and lose their soul without a second thought.

She would know, since she had done just that.

*****

Lisa B. Kamps

Amber "AJ" Johnson is a freelance writer who has her heart set on becoming a full-time sports reporter at her paper. She has one chance to prove herself: capture an interview with the very private goalie of Baltimore's hockey team, Alec Kolchak. But he's the one man who tries her patience, even as he brings to life a quiet passion she doesn't want to admit exists.

Alec has no desire to be interviewed--he never has, never will. But he finds himself a reluctant admirer of AJ's determination to get what she wants...and he certainly never counted on his attraction to her. In a fit of frustration, he accepts AJ's bet: if she can score just one goal on him in a practice shoot-out, he would not only agree to the interview, he would let her have full access to him for a month, 24/7.

It was a bet neither one of them wanted to lose...and a bet neither one could afford to win. But when it came time to take the shot, could either one of them cross the line?

Forensics accountant Bobbi Reeves is pulled back into a world of shadows in order to go undercover as a personal assistant with the Baltimore Banners. Her assignment: get close to defenseman Nikolai Petrovich and uncover the reason he's being extorted. But she doesn't expect the irrational attraction she feels—or the difficulty in helping someone who doesn't want it.

Nikolai Petrovich, a veteran defenseman for the Banners, has no need for a personal assistant—especially not one hired by the team. During the last eight years, he has learned to live simply...and alone. Experience has taught him that letting people close puts them in danger. He doesn't want a personal assistant, and he certainly doesn't need anyone prying into his personal life. But that doesn't stop his physical reaction to the unusual woman assigned to him.

They are drawn together in spite of their differences, and discover a heated passion that neither expected. But when the game is over, will the secrets they keep pull them closer together...or tear them apart?

Kayli Evans lives a simple life, handling the daily operations of her small family farm and acting as the primary care-taker for her fourteen-year-old niece. She knows the importance of enjoying each minute, of living life to its fullest. But she still has worries: about her older brother's safety in the military, about the rift between her two brothers, and about her niece's security and making ends meet. And now there's a new worry she doesn't want: Ian Donovan, her brother's friend.

Ian is a carefree hockey player for the Baltimore Banners who has relatively few worries—until he finds himself suddenly babysitting his seven-year-old nieces for an extended period of time. He has no idea what he's doing, and is thrust even further into the unknown when he's forced to participate in the twins' newest hobby. Meeting Kayli opens a different world for him, a simpler world where family, trust, and love are what matters most.

Baltimore Banners defenseman Randy Michaels has a reputation for hard-hitting, on and off the ice. But he's getting older, and his agent has warned that there are younger, less-expensive players who are eager to take his place on the team. Can his hare-brained idea of becoming a "respectable businessman" turn his reputation around, or has Randy's reputation really cost him the chance of having his contract renewed?

Alyssa Harris has one goal in mind: make the restaurant she's opened with her three friends a success. It's not going to be easy, not when the restaurant is a themed sports bar geared towards women. It's going to be even more difficult because their sole investor is Randy Michaels, her friend's drool-worthy brother who has his own ideas about what makes an interesting menu.

Will the mismatched pair be able to find a compromise as things heat up, both on and off the ice? Or will their differences result in a penalty that costs both of them the game?

Jean-Pierre "JP" Larocque is a speed demon for the Baltimore Banners. He lives for speed off the ice, too, playing fast and loose with cars and women. But is he really a player, or is his carefree exterior nothing more than a show, hiding a lonely man filled with regret as he struggles to forget the only woman who mattered?

Emily Poole thought she knew what she wanted in life, but everything changed five years ago. Now she exists day by day, helping care for her niece after her sister's bitter divorce. It may not be how she envisioned her life, but she's happy. Or so she thinks, until JP re-enters her life. Now she realizes there's a lot more she wants, including a second chance with JP.

Can these two lost souls finally find forgiveness and Break Away to the future? Or will the shared tragedy of their past tear them apart for good this time?

Valerie Michaels knows all about life, responsibility--and hockey. After all, her brother is a defenseman for the Baltimore Banners. The last thing she needs--or wants--is to get tangled up with one of her brother's teammates. She doesn't have time, not when running The Maypole is her top priority. Could that be the reason she's suddenly drawn to the troubled Justin Tome? Or is it because she senses something deeper inside him, something she thinks she can fix?

On the surface, Justin Tome has it all: a successful career with the Banners, money, fame. But he's been on a downward spiral the last few months. He's become more withdrawn, his game has gone downhill, and he's been partying too much. He thinks it's nothing more than what's expected of him, nothing more than once again failing to meet expectations and never quite measuring up. Then he starts dating Val and realizes that maybe he has more to offer than he thinks.

Or does he? Sometimes voices from the past, voices you've heard all your life, are too strong to overcome. And when the unexpected happens, Justin is certain he's looking at a permanent Delay of Game--unless one strong woman can make him see that life is all about the future, not the past.

Sometimes it takes a sinner…

Nicole Taylor has been fighting to get on the right side of the tracks all her life, but never as hard as the last two years. Finally free from an abusive relationship, her focus is on looking forward. Her first step in that direction? A quick get-away to immerse herself in her photography--and a steamy encounter with a gorgeous green-eyed stranger.

To love a saint…

As a forward for The Baltimore Banners, shooting fast and scoring often is just part of the game for Mathias "Mat" Herron. Off the ice is a different story and this off-season, he has a different goal in mind: do whatever it takes to rid himself of the asinine nickname he was recently given by some of his teammates. An encounter with a beautiful stranger helps him do just that.

And life to teach them both what's important…

When reality collides with fantasy, will passion be enough to see them through? Or will it take a shoot-out of another kind to show them what matters most?

Kenny Haskell's hard work and determination finally paid off last season when The Baltimore Banners called him up from the minors. That doesn't mean the quiet defenseman is willing to stop proving himself. Each day is a new fight, a new opportunity, to prove to his coaches, to his team—and to himself—that he belongs with the Banners. Kenny is convinced he'll be able to keep his head in the game with no problems—until he gets thrown out of a youth hockey game by one unforgiving ref who proves to be more of a distraction than he anticipates.

Lauren Gannon approaches life with a single successful mindset: take no prisoners, never give up, and always rely on yourself. At least, that's what she likes to think. The last year has been a little different. Being saddled with her younger sister who refuses to grow up and take responsibility for anything is turning Lauren's world into one crazy disaster after another. The last thing she needs to deal with is a professional hockey player who's too attractive for his own good—or for her sanity.

The one thing Lauren has learned in life is to never underestimate the unexpected, and falling for Kenny definitely fits into that category. Can they really be friends and lovers? Kenny does his best to prove they can. But when a sudden family obligation forces Lauren to choose between what she knows is right and what she thinks is expected, will she find herself skating on thin ice and risking the happiness she really wants?

COACH'S CHALLENGE
A BALTIMORE BANNERS NOVELLA
LISA B. KAMPS

As head coach for The Baltimore Banners, Sonny LeBlanc has seen it all. Guts and glory. Hard-hitting and hard-headed players. A rise to fame and a plummet to failure. Scarred, determined, and tough-as-nails, he's never met a challenge he couldn't conquer—until he meets Monica Jennings.

A single mother who's survived an abusive marriage, Monica Jennings is finally learning to live—little by little. That doesn't mean she's learned to trust and it certainly doesn't mean she's willing to open her heart to anyone but her daughter and her sister. And then she meets Sonny LeBlanc, the scarred coach of The Baltimore Banners. There's something about him that makes her want to take a chance—or run in the other direction and hide.

Can Sonny teach the cautious woman how to embrace love and life, or will he lose it all by calling the riskiest play of his career?

For Dillon Frayser, a rising star for The Baltimore Banners hockey team, life has come easy. A solid childhood, a happy family, a natural talent for playing the game he loves. The only thing missing is the degree he promised his parents he would get soon after he was drafted. If he could just force himself to focus on carbon atoms and organic chemistry, he wouldn't have to worry about squeezing in embarrassing tutoring sessions between a busy schedule filled with practices and games.

Maggie Andersen dreads meeting her new student but she needs the money that tutoring will provide. That doesn't mean she's willing to put up with the anticipated antics of an arrogant brainless jock. When she finally meets Dillon, he turns out to be the exact opposite of what she expected: smart, funny, driven, and humble. Maggie soon finds herself letting her guard down and discovering a different kind of chemistry.

Will the tutoring sessions lead to something more for the mismatched pair? Or is this nothing more than a one-timer for the sexy hockey player?

Jake Evans has been in the Marine Corps for seventeen years, juggling his conflicting duties to country and his teenage daughter. But when he suffers a serious injury and is sent home, he knows he'll be forced to make decisions he doesn't want to. Battered in spirit and afraid of what the future may hold, he takes the long way by driving cross-country.

He never expected to meet Alyce Marshall, a free-spirited woman on a self-declared adventure: she's running away from home.

In spite of her outward free spirit, Alyce has problems of her own she must face, including the ever-present shadow of her father and his influence on her growing up. She senses similarities in Jake, and decides that it's up to her to teach the tough Marine that life isn't just about rules and regulations. What she doesn't plan on is falling in love with him...and being forced to share her secret.

Michaela Donaldson had her whole life planned out: college, music, and a happy-ever-after with her first true love. One reckless night changed all that, setting Michaela on a new path. Gone are her dreams of pursuing music in college, replaced by what she thinks is a more rewarding life. She's a firefighter now, getting down and dirty while doing her job. So what if she's a little rough around the edges, a little too careless, a little too detached? She's happy, living life on her own terms--until Nicky Lansing shows back up.

Nick Lansing was the stereotypical leather-clad bad boy, needing nothing but his fast car, his guitar, his never-ending partying, and his long-time girlfriend--until one bad decision changed the course of two lives forever. He's on the straight-and-narrow now, living life as a respected teacher and doing his best to be a positive role model. Yes, he still has his music. But gone are his days of partying. And gone is the one girl who always held his heart. Or is she?

One freak accident brings these two opposites back together. Is ten years long enough to heal the physical and emotional wounds from the past? Can they reconcile who they were with who they've become--or will it be a case of Once Burned is enough?

Angie Warren was voted the Most Likely to Succeed in school. She was also voted the Most Responsible. And responsible she is: she made it through college on a scholarship and she's even working her way through Vet School. She has an overprotective older brother she adores and a part-time job tending bar that adds some enjoyment to her life. In fact, that's the only pleasure she has. She's bored and in desperate need of a change. Too bad the one guy she has her sights set on is the one guy completely off-limits.

Jay Moore knows all about excitement and wouldn't live life any other way. From his job as a firefighter to his many brief relationships, his whole life is nothing but one thrilling experience after the other. Except when Angie Warren enters the picture. He's known her for years and there is no way he's going to agree to give her the excitement she's looking for. Even Jay knows where to draw the line—and dating his friend's baby sister definitely crosses all of them.

Too bad Angie has other plans. But will either one of them remember that when you're Playing With Fire, someone is bound to get burned?

Dave Warren knows all about protocol. As a firefighter/paramedic, he has to. What he doesn't know is when his life became nothing more than routine, following the rules day in and day out. Has it always been that way, or was it a gradual change? Or did it have anything to do with his time spent overseas as a medic with the Army Reserves? He's not sure, but it's something he's learned to accept and live with—until a series of messages upsets his routine. And until one spitfire Flight Medic enters his life.

Carolann "CC" Covey has no patience for protocols. Yes, they're a necessary evil, a part of her job, but they don't rule her life. She can't let them—she knows life is for the living, a lesson learned the hard way overseas. Which is why her attraction to the serious and staid Dave Warren makes no sense. Is it just a case of "opposites attract", or is it something more? Will CC be able to teach him that sometimes rules need to be broken?

And when something sinister appears from Dave's past to threaten everything he's come to love, will he learn that Breaking Protocol may be the only way to save what's really important?

Dale Gannon has sworn off women. He's seen more than his share of crazy and not all of it has been during his job as a firefighter. His youngest sister, Lindsay, is currently in jail awaiting trial for the attempted poisoning of his other sister, Lauren. Guilt still eats at him, making him wonder if there was something he could have done to prevent Lindsay's fall. Could he have been more supportive? More encouraging? What if…no, he was done with what-ifs. Done with women. Done with people, period. What he needs is peace, quiet…and time to come to grips with everything that's happened in the last six months.

And then he meets the neighbor from hell: a sassy free-spirited woman who quickly turns his life upside down.
Melanie Reeves has always seen things differently, viewing life as an array of color. Bright and vibrant, dark and moody. She captures them, breathes them, gives life to them on canvas. But her obnoxious neighbor is a mystery, one she can't solve, one she can't even read clearly—and one she tries her best to ignore.

Until she discovers the deep guilt that plagues him—guilt he won't admit to or even acknowledge. Can she help him find his way to the surface before the darkness completely engulfs the inner vibrancy she senses in him? Or will he drag her with him into the flames, where they both run the risk of losing who they really are?

Shelby Martin's life is as dry, dull and dusty as the artifacts with which she works, but all that changes when she accepts a dare by her friends: pick up a sexy stranger for one unforgettable night of uncharacteristic passion.

Josh Nichols is a no-nonsense vice cop used to the seedier side of Baltimore. When he's picked up in a bar by Shelby, he realizes the move is out of character for her—and is immediately surprised at the instant chemistry between them. He doesn't count on her disappearing after one hot night—before he gets her full name or even a phone number.

Neither of them expected to see the other again—or to have their worlds turned upside down when they're thrown together as a result of a crime at Shelby's museum. Can two people from completely different worlds look beyond suspicion and build a relationship from one night of unprecedented passion? Or will those differences pull them apart…especially when there's someone else who wants nothing more than to see Shelby fail?